be blessed.

TEMPEST
THE TRAVELER SERIES

BOOK 1

JUDITH K. GALLAGHER AND V.C. WARREN

DEDICATIONS

To my husband, Jim, and the five J's, who encouraged me to have the courage to cross the bridge and begin the journey. *Judith K. Gallagher*

To my husband, Jake, whose faith in me has never faltered. You are my inspiration and my hero, and I thank God for bringing me to you. *V.C. Warren*

ACKNOWLEDGMENTS

Thanks to John Gallagher for the cover photograph of Judith K. Gallagher.

Thanks to Patti Vorwick of Patti Vorwick Photography for the cover photograph of V.C. Warren.

Thanks to our families for allowing us time away to cross the bridge with Nick often and at length. This would have been impossible without your patience and understanding.

Thanks to God for orchestrating our meeting, crafting our friendship, and making us sisters of the heart.

PROLOGUE:
THE EDICT

The old scribe massaged his weary hand before picking up the quill. Steadying a tremor that was worsening with every year, he dipped the pen in the bowl of ink and squinted down in the flickering light at the scroll. His reading glasses had been lost long ago, but the words of the Edict were carved into his mind's eye, which remained clear. They were the same words he always wrote. Scroll after scroll. Year after year. The words that filled his waking hours and haunted his dreams. The words that were his reality. Few things were left to his imagination. Things such as wondering where each scroll would end up: hanging on the side of a barn; nailed to a post; tacked to a tree; plastered beside a busy doorway; or crumpled and forgotten in a dusty corner. And those souls mistaken for Travelers, he wondered about them, too. They, in particular, occupied his thoughts. He invented lives for them as he wrote. Imagination was his only escape from the dreary, gray room in which he spent his days. Scowling, the old man forced his hand to write the familiar words:

From the Keeper of the Third Bridge with respect to the Gathering of the Shades:

It is to my great and lofty regret that I must proclaim, once again, that the Citizens of Tempest remain, as always, woefully, fearfully, and negligently remiss in the Gathering of Shades. Your continued remissness is such that I am forced, once again, to impose more severe tariffs, stricter rations, and harsher Rules of Business. Remember, Citizens, this is due to no cause of mine, but is a result of your very own negligence.

Also remember this: Each Shade gathered not only lines the pockets of an honorable Crimp, it increases the Fleet. And increasing the Fleet increases the chances of harvesting a True Traveler, something which is, of course, our ultimate aim.

As always: For the man or child (or woman, if possible) who brings me the hand of a Traveler, I bequeath the sum of Fifteen Hundred Thousand Plunkets, in addition to a generous but reasonable reduction of tariffs, and removal of Provisions 3 and 11 of the Rules of Business.

BRING ME THE HAND OF A TRAVELER!!

/CFS

CHAPTER 1

CRAZY CARLOTA'S BRIDGE
BETWEEN WORLDS

"I f he's not dead, then where is he?"

His question was answered not by his Grandma Carlota, but by something lukewarm and slightly slimy bouncing off the back of his neck.

Nick Sanchez braced himself. He'd already sworn a silent oath that if he was hit again, he would retaliate instead of sitting there taking hit after repulsive hit. But he did take it, and he was still sitting. So, instead, he renewed his vow to himself. He pretended to focus on his grandma, but his muscles, his mind, his pulse trembled in anticipation of a coming explosion that had been building for weeks.

Ignorant of the war being waged around her, the old woman sitting next to him laid a hand on his arm. "Nicco," Carlota said in that thick accent he was still trying to get used to, "perhaps I would tell you if you asked for the right reason. Now, look at this one."

Simmering at the quiet admonishment, he lowered his gaze as if he were looking at the pages of the photo album spread across her lap. Instead, he studied her hands, so pale and veined they looked inhuman. It was only one of the reasons he didn't like touching her or her touching him. Another was because he had only a vague memory of this woman who was his grandmother. She was as foreign to him as his own father, Dr. Miguel Sanchez — better known as Mike.

Speaking of whom, Nick eyed the door and let his resentment seep out in one long sigh. Mike had once again made himself scarce.

Nick had only been living with his father for five weeks, and for five consecutive Wednesdays, they had driven across town just so Mike could visit with his mother, Carlota. Carlota's world consisted of a dreary room furnished with used hospital furniture in a depressing one-story building called Fountain Creek Assisted Living. The whole place made you think of gray even when you were looking at the red plastic geraniums lining the sidewalk.

For five consecutive Wednesdays, Mike had mumbled a greeting to his wrinkled mother then made some lame excuse and disappeared for an hour. Each "visit" was then followed by a silent ride back across town, a miserable trip which concluded with Mike being in a foul mood for two solid days.

Nick couldn't say that the weekly visits did much to improve his own mood either. So far, sour moods were the only thing he and Mike seemed to have in common.

"Mike didn't wear his necklace today," Nick said. It was the first time he'd seen his father without the gold chain peeking out of the neck of his shirt. He knew the necklace had been a gift from Mike's long absent father. Disappointed by his grandma's lack of a response, he added, "Did you notice?"

Carlota frowned. Her only other reaction was to jab him in the ribs with a knobby elbow. "Look at your grandpapa. He is handsome, no?"

Nick glanced at the grainy photograph. Despite not wanting to care, he couldn't help being curious. All his life, he'd heard rumors of Grandpa Fidel, the man who'd run off and left Grandma Carlota to raise Nick's father alone. He'd learned quickly, without having to be told, that Fidel was a forbidden subject in Mike's presence. Personally, Nick figured the old man was dead, which had prompted his question.

Carlota tipped her head to the side and studied Nick with dark eyes shrouded behind a veil of bifocals and sagging eyelids. "You look like him, I think." She patted his leg gently.

He frowned and slid away from the invasive hand. "I don't think so."

Brooking no argument, she nodded. "I see it in the eyes and the hair." Carlota sighed and glanced back at the picture, her smile as faded as the image. "My Fidel is a good man."

Nick shrugged. Based on what little he knew about his grandfather, he'd have to disagree. On top of that, Fidel didn't look all that handsome to him. He looked grouchy and mean, like an angrier, heavier, balder version of Mike.

Nick tugged on his own thick, black hair. Cropped short in the back, the front hung down over his eyes. While Mike hadn't said anything about Nick's hair or the lip ring, he knew both annoyed his father. He'd lost count of the times he'd caught Mike staring at them. In fact, he'd begun to enjoy running his tongue over the circle of metal whenever he felt his father's eyes on him. He wasn't about to tell Mike the ring was just a clip that he pulled off when he was in private.

That pinched, offended look Mike wore when he eyed the ring made the secret worthwhile.

Grandma Carlota leaned forward to squint down at another photo that had caught her eye when the enemy struck again. Something tepid and prickly hit Nick on the back of the head then dropped onto the collar of his jacket — his brand new leather jacket. Enough was enough.

He shot off the bed and spun around. Carlota's room-mate, a wrinkled old woman who smelled like a pile of stale, dirty laundry, lay curled under the blankets on her bed. To the unsuspecting, she was sleeping, but Nick knew better. He watched until she peered at him over a tray of half-eaten dinner. The old hag had a habit of stashing pieces of food under her pillow then lobbing them at Nick when no one was looking. She'd been doing it since his very first visit. In another place and time, if it had been happening to someone else, it might have been funny, but Nick had left his sense of humor sprawled like a flattened skunk on the tarmac at O'Hare airport five weeks and three days ago.

Frowning, he lifted a hand to his collar and wrapped his fingers around a chunk of over-cooked broccoli. Nick held up the limp shrapnel to the sound of a creepy giggle. "Listen, you old crow-"

"Nicco!" Carlota gasped.

He turned on his grandmother. "And for the last time, my name is Nick!"

He flung the decomposing broccoli back at the old hag then stomped out of the room and ran to the visitors lounge, because he didn't know where else to go. Thankfully, the small room was empty. It looked as if someone had tried to decorate it sometime in the past. Now, the faded floral wallpaper curling in the corners simply added to the air of hopelessness that the residents breathed in every day. The room boasted three vending machines that shook worse than Carlota's hands, and four little tables with metal chairs. The tables wobbled and the chairs screamed like terrified girls when you scooted them across the tile floor.

Still angry, Nick dug in his pockets and sorted through a handful of change. Not enough for a soda, and the stupid machines in this old west town didn't take credit cards. He glanced over his shoulder at the hallway then fed the machine until it spat out a paper cup with spindly cardboard handles shaped like butterfly wings. A spray of dark liquid shot mostly into the cup, the rest splattering onto the tiles in explanation of the half-moon stain on the floor near his feet. The machine belched before emitting a final hiss of steam.

Sloshing more hot coffee onto the tiles, Nick pulled out the cup and started to take a sip. The smell stopped him. It reminded him of the formaldehyde-laced frogs in the biology room at school. Coughing back a gag, he pulled out a squalling chair and sat down at the table nearest the door. His chair rocked on uneven legs as he cradled the hot cup in his hands.

He hated this place. And by "this place," he didn't mean just this building reeking of old people and cleaning fluids that failed to disguise the smell of vomit and pee.

He hated Colorado Springs.

He hated living with his dad.

He even hated his mom.

After all, she was the one who'd sent him here; she'd claimed he was too much to handle. "Right. Sure, I am," he snorted to himself.

He'd had a lot of good friends in Chicago. Cool guys who always stuck by him even though they sometimes got a little rough or did things he didn't always agree with. Going along with their ideas and schemes wasn't a bad price to pay for their acceptance. His mom had no right to ship him off to his dad without asking him if he wanted to go. He hadn't even known that his mom and dad had gone back to court to change the custody agreement until it was all over, until some judge had already signed him over to a virtual stranger. Even with the frequent fights he and his mom had, he'd never seen it coming. She'd blindsided him, and there wasn't anything he could do about it.

Nick sighed. His life sucked, and it would be four years before he could get out on his own. A lifetime away.

"Aren't you a little young for coffee?"

Startled to discover he wasn't alone, Nick swung around to look at the table in the back corner. It was the weird nurse with the wild red hair and long, horse-like face. Each week when he and Mike came for their visit, the woman was there. Every time he turned around, she was silently staring at him over her crooked nose. Nick felt the hair on the back of his neck stand up like a wary dog. He could have sworn the room was empty and was glad he was between her and the door.

"I've been watching you," she said as if she'd read his mind.

Nick raised his cup and took a small slurp of the foul coffee just to prove he wasn't too young for it. That he wasn't freaked out by her sudden appearance. It tasted worse than it smelled, and it was all he could do to not grimace as he set the cup on the table. He drummed up the same false courage he used when his friends pulled a wild prank. "Yeah, it's a little hard not to notice. So, what's your problem anyway?"

When the nurse chuckled, Nick could have sworn her horse-face flickered like an old movie. Then her smile snapped off like a light bulb, and she stood up. "At this particular moment, Nicholas Sanchez, you're my problem."

Nick stood up, too. He wasn't sure why except that he thought he might have to run back the way he'd come. But before he did, he took a moment to really, really look at her. Green eyes sparkled beneath over-plucked eyebrows, and shy cheekbones crouched behind a thick layer of blush. Her oversized head was out of sorts with her petite body, and her long arms ended in abrupt, stubby fingers. Her bony bits — elbows, wrists and knuckles — looked hard and sharp as marble, and her pale skin was as smooth and polished as cuttlebone. Her frizzy hair was held back from her face by plastic lady bug barrettes that matched the insect pattern on her uniform. She could have been younger than Mike or older than Grandma Carlota. When his gaze finally settled on her thin lips, her statement suddenly reached his brain.

Tension coiling like a spring inside him, Nick reached down and wrapped one hand around the hot, flimsy cup.

He could use the scalding liquid as a weapon if he had to. "How'd you know my name?"

She shrugged. "Would you like to know mine?"

His tongue toying with his lip ring, Nick shrugged back. "Whatever."

"Whatever," she grinned. "I like that. Whatever." She shoved her short fingers into the pockets of her scrubs. "It's Miriam."

"So?" He lowered his head until his eyes were hidden behind by a thick hairy wall of bangs.

Miriam sighed and seemed to settle into herself, shrinking a bit. "The men in your family are exceedingly," she paused, tapping a long, narrow shoe on the tile floor, "difficult."

"You know my dad?"

"Miguel. Yes, I know him."

Miguel? Only Grandma called Mike by his real name. That must be how the nurse knew their names. She'd been talking to Carlota. His grip on the cup eased slightly.

"And Fidel. Although, I've haven't seen him for quite some time." She shook her head, her lady bug barrettes bouncing as if they were struggling to fly away. "It's quite unfortunate that situation."

"You know my grandfather?" Now he knew she was crazy.

"You don't believe me?" One hand came out from the scrub pocket and a fingernail traced a pattern in the cookie crumbs left stranded on the table.

Nick smirked. "Where is he then?"

Sharp green eyes studied him. "Perhaps I would tell you if you asked for the right reason."

"Right," he mumbled, thinking how menacing his grandma's words sounded coming out of this stranger's mouth. He wondered if Miriam was intentionally trying to scare him.

She lifted her hands as if in surrender. "Okay, okay. I'll play nice."

When she stepped towards him, he matched her by stepping back. Other than not liking anyone in his personal space, he wasn't sure why he did it, because he didn't think she was necessarily dangerous, just eerie and disturbing. The nurse stopped and gave him a sad smile.

"I'm sorry, Nicholas. I wish I could tell you what you want to know. It just isn't...well, it's not permitted."

"Listen, lady-"

"Miriam."

He shook his head. "Whatever your name is. Listen, I probably shouldn't even be talking to you."

"Why?"

He wasn't sure, except that he didn't want to talk to her. "Because you're probably a stalker or a child molester or something." When she frowned, he explained, "You're always staring at me. Creeping around following me."

"I don't creep, but I had to be sure first."

"Be sure of what?"

"That you'd take it."

The woman was seriously messed up, and his face must have conveyed what he was thinking because she sighed again, loudly. "Look, I know it goes against your nature, Nicholas, but you're going to have to trust me." Ignoring his ill-mannered skeptical grunt, she held out her right hand, palm up. Something gold glittered on it. As she cautiously approached him, Nick couldn't help staring at the object in her hand, even though everything in him was telling him to retreat.

"What is it?" It looked like a coin, a foreign one with lots of strange symbols and writing. When she didn't answer, he looked from the object to the woman. "You want me to take it?"

"Not if you don't want to."

Hesitantly, Nick reached out and picked up the strange piece of metal. On its center were written the words "Pontis

Viator." Surrounding the center, rows of raised symbols formed two rings around the outside edge. He looked at her again. "It's some kind of coin."

Miriam stared back at him. "Do you accept it?"

He studied it again. It was unlike anything he'd ever seen. He shrugged, pretending nonchalance. "What's the catch?"

"The catch?"

"Yeah. You know, what's it going to cost me?"

Miriam smiled and once again, he would have sworn her image flickered. "The cost has been paid in full, Nicholas."

"By?" When she didn't answer, he added, "Nothing's ever free."

She shook her head slightly, her frizzy hair lifting with sudden static as lady bugs reached for the ceiling. "All in due time. Knowledge comes only with learning."

It sounded like mumbo-jumbo. "So, you're telling me the coin's free? You're just going to give it to me?"

"No." The horse-face grew serious. "No, the cube is far from free. It is, in fact, invaluable. The price paid intolerable. But, yes, all you have to do is accept it."

She made about as much sense as geometry. She referred to a coin as a cube and talked about something not costing anything but not being free. Still, it sounded like he might walk away from this deal with what could be a valuable coin and he wasn't going to have to pay for it. Miriam was kind of creepy, but he really only had to see her once a week at the most. He could probably avoid her most of the time. It didn't seem like he had much to lose.

"Okay. Sure, why not? If it'll make you happy and you'll quit following me around, I'll take it." He started to put it in his pocket, but she grabbed him, wrapping squat fingers around his wrist as the coin warmed his palm.

"Sic, Dominus," she hissed. "Say it."

"What?"

"Sic, Dominus. You must say it." Her grip on his arm tightened.

Nick was already starting to regret his decision. "Why?"

"It's the only way." Green eyes studied him. "Sic, Dominus," she repeated.

"Sic..." He cleared his throat of hesitation. "Sic, Dominus."

Miriam laughed softly and her grip eased, but she didn't let go. Then she looked down at the coin and murmured, "Infinitas, to your rightful owner at last." This time, her image really did flicker. Her hair and the edges of her long face wavered, faded, and then came back. Nick tried to pull away, but her hold on him was surprisingly strong. Her gaze lifted to his face, holding him as surely as her short-fingered hand. "Your blessings will be great, Nicholas Sanchez, but your hardships will be greater, for there are pathways not even the falcon's eye has seen or the storm taken." Miriam leaned so close their noses touched. Her green eyes peered deep into his brown ones. "But, there is a Watcher always. Remember this, Traveler, and it will ease your crossings."

She let go of him and Nick stepped back, bumping the table and sloshing coffee. The coin or the cube or whatever you wanted to call it was still wrapped in his fist. Miriam flickered, the air around her crackled softly. He opened his mouth to ask her what was going on, or maybe just to scream a little, but she cut him off.

"I must leave you for now." She darted past him towards the hallway, but then stopped and looked back. "Speak to Carlota. She knows more than she knows." The air around her buzzing, Miriam's horse-face darkened. "And, Nicholas, beware the elected one." She turned and was gone.

Nick stood. Not thinking. Not feeling. Just standing there with coffee dripping onto his best sneakers, his mind a blank, and his heart hammering in his chest. He blinked twice before his brain rebooted.

The coin hot in his hand, he heard shoes clicking on the tiled floor. In a daze, he stepped out of the visitors lounge and glanced down the hallway. A pudgy nurse in a white uniform was pushing a cart. He looked the other way. An old man in a wheelchair was pulling himself down the hall using the handrail. But no Miriam. No red-haired, witchy-looking, horse-faced woman.

Maybe he'd lost his mind.

Maybe he'd been drugged. He squinted warily down at the coffee.

Barely glancing at the coin, he slipped it into his pocket, pitched the coffee into the trash, and walked slowly back to Carlota's room. She was sitting where he'd left her — perched on her bed leafing through the photo album balanced on her bony lap. For the first time, he noticed she wore the same pink scuffs and floral-print dress every week.

As if he had never left the room and encountered a crazy woman, Carlota patted the bed beside her and said, "Come."

Nick eyed the nasty neighbor who was now lying on her bed facing the window, pretending to sleep. Then he looked out at the brightly lit corridor where old people shuffled past or rolled by in wheelchairs pushed by scowling nurses. Not wanting to, he entered the room. His pulse pounded incessantly against his temples as he sat next to his grandma on the beige bedspread.

"Where's Mike?" he managed.

Carlota frowned over at him. "He is your father. You should not call him by his name. It is disrespectful."

Nick shrugged, but otherwise didn't answer. Why should he respect a man he barely knew? What had Mike ever done for him? He nodded down at the photos, his heart and brain still racing as he tried to understand what had just happened, and what he had — or had not — just seen. "Mike never talks about his father."

"He does not," she agreed, "but he wears the prayer necklace his papa gave him. Always." She frowned a little and said, "Except today."

Nick cleared his throat. "Is it because his dad ran off and left you when Mike was just a kid? Is that why he doesn't talk about him?"

He jumped when Carlota slammed the album closed. She inhaled through her nose, her nostrils flaring as she stared at him with her lips pressed together in a rigid line. "I will tell you a secret about your grandpapa." She glanced over her shoulder at her roommate. Then apparently satisfied they were not being spied on, she leaned close, making him uncomfortable. "He is special."

Nick didn't know what to say, so he didn't say anything. He held himself stiffly, forcing himself not to pull away as Carlota continued.

"Fidel is not like us. He travels."

He frowned. Miriam had just called him a Traveler; she claimed to know his Grandpa Fidel. Carlota's lips brushed his ear, startling him.

"To other worlds," she whispered.

Nick glanced up at the doorway opening onto the corridor. He wondered where Mike was and if he was going to return soon. He wondered where Miriam had gone and what or who Miriam really was. Maybe his mom had been right. She'd always said Grandma Carlota was crazy. Nick started to slide off the bed to go in search of Mike as his mind argued against any connection between Miriam's and his grandmother's words.

For the second time today, he was stopped by a woman with a surprisingly strong hand. "I know what they say about me," Carlota snarled, twisted fingers clutching the sleeve of his jacket. "But, I am not crazy. I am not! I saw him do it. Once. When he did not know I was watching."

Nick frowned, hyper-aware of the coin weighing down his left front pocket. "I should go find Mike," he mumbled.

"He folds space. I do not know how he does it, but he does."

"Folds space?"

Carlota grinned and nodded. "Yes. That is what he said when he found out I had seen. I remember clearly, Nicco. He spoke of a bridge between folded space."

"But that—" He started to say that didn't make sense, but he stopped when Carlota looked up at the doorway. He followed her gaze.

Mike was standing in the open door. As ambivalent as he felt about his father, even Nick had to admit that there was something compelling about Mike Sanchez. Head professor of the Geology Department at a local university, Mike was not only very intelligent, he was handsome and well-liked. He had a smile and a way about him that Nick envied; he garnered respect from apparently everybody but Nick; he was easy-going and genuine.

But right now, Mike looked anything but easy-going. His skin was unnaturally flushed and charcoal eyes flashed in anger. "What are you doing?"

"Uh, we were just talking," Nick murmured, but Mike wasn't looking at him.

"We were just talking," Carlota mimicked with an innocent smile. "Come, sit down and join us, son."

Nick felt something bounce off the back of his head. Grandma's roommate was once again using him for target practice, but he ignored her, focusing instead on Mike who stood frozen in place.

"I told you I didn't want you telling him those ignorant lies." Mike's tone was as sharp as his words.

"Your papa is coming back, Miguel. You must believe that."

The anger in Mike's face drained into a look of resigned defeat. "Mother, please," he pleaded, and even though Nick didn't understand what was going on, he felt a little sorry for his dad.

"He has not abandoned us," Carlota mumbled.

Mike pulled his car keys from his pocket. "It's time to go."

Nick lowered himself off the bed, but Carlota still had a grip on him. She was watching Mike, tears gathering in the corners of her eyes. "Your papa will come back. He promised."

"Nicco, come on." Mike stalked away, headed for the parking lot. Nick knew he should follow, but he hesitated. He always dreaded these visits, but now he wished he had more time. He wanted to show Carlota the coin, and he wanted to find Miriam. He needed to know if what he thought he'd seen had really happened or whether the flickering had been a mere trick of the florescent light.

"Fidel promised he would always come back, and he will. When he can. I know he will."

Nick looked over at his grandma who stared back at him. Gently, he pried himself free of her grasp. "Sure he will, Grandma," he heard himself saying.

A change came over her at his words. She sat up straighter and her eyes brightened. "Really?"

Nick ignored a fuzzy clump of cold broccoli that arched over his grandma's bed and hit him on the chest. "Yeah," he said, even though he wasn't sure he meant it or why he said it. "Really."

CHAPTER 2

A BRIDGE TO SOMEWHERE

Nick groaned as they pulled into the driveway: the housekeeper was here. It wasn't that he cared whether Rosa was working. After all, during the short time he'd been here, they had developed a mutual disregard which suited him just fine. It was just that, unfortunately, Rosa's daughter, Jo, wasn't as easy to ignore.

With a soft, uncharacteristic curse, Mike edged around Rosa's dented 1973 Olds that blocked the garage door like a goalie at the World Cup. Shooting a sideways glance at his already irritated father, Nick hopped out before the car came to a complete stop and strode into the house leaving the passenger door hanging open.

"Nick, get back here," Mike ordered. "Close the door!"

Ignoring the command, Nick headed towards his room, snorting under his breath when he heard both car doors slam shut. Typical. His dad never followed through on anything when it came to his son.

In the family room, the vacuum cleaner hummed as Rosa sang out snatches of an unfamiliar song. Shrugging off his jacket, Nick let it drop to the floor, kicked his door shut with one foot, and turned on his computer. Then he paced, studying the coin as he waited for the computer to boot.

The dull surface and ancient etchings on the coin evoked a strange restlessness in him, probably because he was still disturbed by his encounter with Miriam. It had left him with the vague impression that his life had changed, but he didn't know how. He glanced at his closed door, listening to the footsteps passing rapidly down the hall. Nick smirked when Mike moved past his room without even a stutter in his long-legged stride.

He'd known there was no likelihood of an argument with his dad. Within the first half hour after he'd landed at the Denver airport, he'd figured out his dad would do almost anything to avoid conflict with him. Mike avoided physical contact as well. After an initial awkward, one-armed hug and pat on the back, avoidance had become Mike's favored technique. It had become a game to Nick to see just how far he could push his dad.

As for his mom — well, she didn't avoid conflict. She met it head-on, screaming at the top of her lungs. And until she'd shocked him by shipping him off to the middle of nowhere, Nick had never had any problem figuring her out. He knew exactly which buttons to push, where the line was. At least that's what he had thought.

Nick took a deep breath then let it hiss out between clenched teeth, tapping his fist against the corner of the desk as he got mad all over again. He'd never had a problem figuring out where his mom stood on anything until she'd snuck back to court, had the custody changed, and without a word of warning changed his life forever.

A door slammed shut down the hallway, punctuating the fact that Mike wasn't going to confront him. That was fine with Nick; the less he had to say to Mike, the better. Who needed words? Slamming doors said everything that needed to be said.

Sitting down at the desk, Nick shoved aside the clutter of school books, comics, balled-up wrappers, and crumpled cellophane. He licked his fingertips, wetting them to gather stray crumbs from the desktop. As he licked off a mixture of chocolate, potato chips, and dried cake, he rubbed the strange coin with his other hand, picking at the raised design with his fingernail. Half-heartedly, he turned his attention to the computer and waded through a couple of websites on old coins. 'Infinitas.' That was what the crazy lady had called it. He typed the word into the search engine, hoping for a match. Nothing. Maybe he was spelling it wrong.

"There has to be something," he muttered. "Maybe under Spanish golden doubloons."

The results were frustrating. There were so many websites, it would take a year to search through all of them, and after a few more attempts, he gave up. Staring at the computer, he thought about his grandma's cryptic words: 'He travels...to other worlds.'

Carlota was crazy. Now that he wasn't looking into her tear-filled eyes, there was no doubt about that. And that Miriam woman? She was crazier. "Crazy must be contagious," he mumbled. "I've gotta be nuts to waste my time with this." He leaned back, staring at the screen, his thoughts twisting and tumbling like his screen saver. Maybe the crazies were somehow connected. Like a bridge.

He scooted forward and typed 'folds space' into the search engine. Surprised by the number of websites that came up, he scrolled through the long list. There were sites for science fiction shows, free screen savers, pinball machines, and furniture. There were several hits for a movie and online videos. He didn't see anything about coins or cubes. He clicked on a site about warping space and followed a link to wormholes and time. As the webpage downloaded, he looked at the coin again.

Pontis Viator. He rubbed the raised letters with his thumb.

An irritating tapping interrupted his thoughts. Gritting his teeth, Nick tried to ignore it as he began his inspection of the website. The tapping increased in a tuneless pattern as if someone were playing the door in lieu of a piano. Much to his annoyance, Nick realized his fingers had joined the concert and were drumming along. Why was everyone trying to get in his head today? He balled his fists in his lap just as the door flew open.

Jo stood in the doorway coiling a strand of her long, dark hair around one finger. The slender girl completely ignored Nick's scowl as he snapped, "Ever hear of privacy?"

She gave him a one-shoulder shrug. "You ever hear of locking the door if you don't want someone to open it?" Reaching into her pocket, she pulled out a pack of gum. Exchanging the fresh piece for the wad already in her mouth, she sealed the used piece in the gum wrapper and shot a perfect arc into the waste can beside Nick's desk. "Two points," she crowed in a mock whisper, "and the crowd goes wild."

In her normal voice, Jo said, "Privacy, huh? Who are you, Howard Hughes?"

"Howard Hughes? Who's that?"

Jo was the only person he knew who could roll her eyes without actually rolling her eyes. It was an indefinable cockiness in her stance and the tilt of her head. "You know, a filthy rich recluse?" When he didn't respond, she shook her head then looked around at the cluttered floor. "They didn't teach you much in Chicago, did they? Like who Howard Hughes was and about this wonderful new invention called a laundry basket." She nudged his new jacket with her foot. "And coat hangers. They don't have them in the Windy City?"

Her eyes became fixed on something next to his unmade bed. She raised one eyebrow, leading him to turn around to see what she was looking at. A pair of dirty boxer shorts.

"Polka dots?" She smirked. "Is that the latest in gangsta' wear this season?" She rocked her slim shoulders back and forth as she swaggered into the room, mocking him with an exaggerated strut.

Nick's face burned. His mouth opened, but he couldn't think of anything to say. "Shut up," he finally spat, his teeth clenched. Of all the rotten, irritating things that he'd had to deal with since moving in with his dad, Jo Torres was one of the most frustrating.

She was cute, but not in a 'you don't stand a chance unless you're first string Varsity' way. Just cute enough for him to have wanted to get some private time with her when Mike had introduced them. The first chance he'd had, Nick had casually wrapped his arm around Jo's shoulders. That had been a mistake.

The bruise on his ribs had only recently faded, testament that Jo could take care of herself. Her elbow had perfect aim, and he assumed she was just as adept at using her fists and knees. Then she'd opened her mouth…

Jo wielded words like a samurai with a sword, and she wasn't the least bit impressed with what she called Nick's gangsta' act. Fortunately, once she'd started talking, any attraction to her that he might have felt had plummeted. Obviously, the feeling was mutual.

"Get out of here and leave me alone. I've got stuff to do." He emphasized the word stuff, hoping she'd be intimidated and leave him alone.

She wasn't. "Stuff as in homework? Or stuff as in video games?" She walked over to peer at the screen. Nick minimized it, but not quickly enough. "Folded space?" Jo commented. "Doesn't sound like any biology homework I've ever heard of. And what's an Einstein-Rosen bridge?"

"Nothing you need to know about."

"Probably not," she agreed, "especially if it's somewhere you're going. What's it got to do with folding space anyway?"

Jo was smart, and Nick wasn't ready to banter with her about something he didn't understand. His eyes narrowed. "The only folding space you need to worry about is a place to do the laundry. Why don't you pick up the dirty clothes and get out of my room? I think that's what my dad is paying you for."

Jo's gum chewing stopped, and for a full double count she simply stared at him. Her lips pursed and a tiny bubble of gum appeared then snapped into nonexistence with a sound like a face being slapped. "For your information, he's not paying me anything. He pays my mom." Her chin lifted and her brown eyes flashed. "And the fact that you're thinking at all is a scary event." Before Nick could reply, she spun and walked out of the room, leaving the door wide open. "Pick up your own dirty clothes, especially those polka-dotted undies," she ordered as she headed towards the kitchen.

For a moment, Nick felt victorious. It was rare for him to come anywhere close to winning a fight with Jo. But his sense of pride was short-lived when it dawned on him that even though she drove him crazy, Jo was the closest thing to a friend that he had here. As lame as that sounded, it was true. She teased him and didn't hesitate to laugh at him, but she wasn't particularly cruel. Some days, she was the only one who spoke to him at school, leading him to the conclusion that even taunts were better than silence.

Self-pity swamped pride as he realized how pathetic his life had become. He pounded the desk with his fist in frustration. He felt rotten about his life, and he wanted everyone around him to feel as bad as he did. Jo, Mike, Carlota...whoever was a convenient target.

Mentally daring anyone else to darken his door, Nick looked back at the computer, quickly scanning an article about wormholes and spatial shortcuts that he didn't understand. It wasn't surprising considering that Albert Einstein's name appeared several times in the article. After all, he might not know who Howard Hughes was, but he knew about Einstein. He was the brainiac with the weird hair who had lived a long time ago and had something to do with the theory of relativity — something else Nick couldn't grasp.

"Einstein-Rosen Bridge," he mumbled as he noticed the heading that Jo had pointed out. It was hard to wade through the scientific jargon, but apparently, Einstein and another guy named Nathan Rosen had believed a black hole, or a bridge, could connect two places in space, making it possible to travel from one dimension to another.

"What are you looking at?"

He jumped and looked over his shoulder. Mike was standing in the doorway, the doorway Jo had left open when she'd stormed out. "Uh...." Nick's brain scrambled for an answer. He knew Mike didn't like discussing anything Grandma Carlota had to say, and the subject of Grandpa Fidel would really set him off.

Normally, Nick would have jumped at an opportunity to goad his dad, but this felt different — like he'd been caught doing something wrong. Then, before he could minimize the window on the monitor, Mike walked over and leaned close. Blinking up through the hair covering his eyes, Nick saw the image of the black hole reflected in his dad's glasses.

He swallowed dryly as Mike said, "Einstein-Rosen Bridge?" His dad turned his head, looking at Nick much like Jo had a few moments ago, with an odd combination of confusion and anger and hurt. "Why are you researching the Einstein-Rosen Bridge theory?"

Mike said it with a voice of authority, like he knew what it was. A little surprised, Nick turned back to the computer and shrugged. He couldn't think of a plausible lie, so he blurted out the truth. "I was thinking about what Grandma Carlota said about Grandpa folding space. I was just—"

"Just what?" Mike's expression hardened, and Nick experienced a moment of doubt as he wondered if he'd misjudged this man he barely knew. "I thought I told you to ignore her. I warned you that she'd try and suck you in to her ridiculous stories. Her delusions." His voice rising, Mike said, "Why can't you just listen for once?"

"I–I was just curious," Nick stammered, caught off guard by the angry accusation. He'd gotten used to his father's habit of avoiding confrontation. This was a stranger who didn't appear to have any trouble sharing his opinion.

"Well, don't be," Mike snapped. "It's a stupid theory, and anyone who believes you can travel to other dimensions through a black hole is simply ignorant." He straightened and pointed a neatly manicured finger. "Get one thing straight, Nick. My father left us. He left your grandmother, and he left me, and my mother has never been able to accept the simple fact that her husband abandoned her. That's all there is to it. He didn't care enough about his family to stick around. It may be an ugly fact of life, but it makes a whole lot more sense than traveling across invisible bridges." Mike took a deep breath and stared beyond Nick. "Turn off the computer."

"No." The word seemed a whole lot bigger than it was. It filled the entire room, but it was now or never. Nick crossed his arms, leaned back in his chair and stared up at his dad with what he hoped was a smug grin plastered on his face. "I'm not finished." He waited for Mike to back down and leave like he always did.

The brash smile faltered and time slowed to a crawl as his dad stared back at him. "Yes, you are," Mike said quietly as he bent down and pulled the plug on the computer.

There was a momentary hum then the monitor went black. Anger surged through him as if the electricity that had fed his computer had been rerouted to his veins. "Are you nuts? You'll fry the hard-drive!" That probably wasn't true, but it sounded serious.

Mike's response was calm, but firm. "Then you'll pay for it yourself, or live without a computer. Either way, you're going to do what I say."

Nick felt something shift between him and his dad, and he didn't like it. He gave an ugly snort and his own voice rose like his dad's had just moments ago. "Right, and I'm going to do that because..."

Suddenly, Mike looked tired and old. "Because whether you like it or not, I'm your father."

His chair scraped the floor as Nick shot up. "Yeah? So where have you been all these years? You sure aren't much of a father, are you? What, are you an expert at long distance parenting?" Nick could see each word making contact with his dad like a solid body shot.

Mike took a step back. "Ni-Nicco," he faltered.

"I guess as long as you sent Mom the check every month, you figured you were doing your bit to raise me, huh?"

"That's not fair." Mike pulled his reading glasses off and rubbed his eyes. "I know this probably isn't what you wanted, but your mom...." Nick grunted, but Mike ignored him and continued, slowly choosing his words as if he were tiptoeing through a mine field. "Your mom and I have always tried to do what was best for you. Even now. Coming here."

"Right. It was a game of custody between you and Mom, and you lost." Hands clenched at his side, Nick hissed, "I feel sorry for you." Resentment consumed him, and he wanted nothing more than to be able to impress upon Mike what a rotten father he'd been. As he searched for the right words to fling, he heard a soft gasp.

Mike and Nick turned towards the sound. Jo and her mother were standing in the hall outside the open door. Jo's frown and the shocked look on Rosa's face left little doubt that they had not only witnessed the argument, but weren't happy about it.

"What are you staring at?" Nick demanded.

Mike's face reddened. "Rosa," he said quietly, "why don't you go home early today."

In her heavily accented English, Rosa answered quietly, "But, Señor Sanchez, the house is not yet finished. The laundry," she gestured towards the clothes littering Nick's floor.

Mike shook his head and gave a little wave. "It's okay." His voice was soft and strained. "You can take care of it next time. Just go on home. Your check's on my desk."

Rosa nodded, embarrassment etched in her face. "Sí." She stepped aside as Mike pushed past her without another word. "Come, Josefina." With a quick look at Nick, she turned and walked rapidly down the hall with Jo close on her heels.

Nick was still standing there a minute later when Jo's head popped around the doorway. "What's it feel like to be a complete and total jerk?" she snapped. "You don't know how good you've got it, you know." She started to leave then stopped. "Don't forget to slam your door. And maybe this time you better lock it." Before he could answer, she disappeared.

Nick stared at the empty hall. His face was hot, like he'd been slapped. The anger that had fueled his outburst was melting like ice cream dumped on a hot sidewalk. In the distance, he heard doors shut and a car engine start as Jo and her mother left.

He was more alone than he'd ever been in his life.

"I hate this place," he declared and kicked his jacket across the room. It landed like a leather exclamation point across the foot of his bed.

Frowning, Nick toyed with his lip ring. Jo was wrong. Why was he the jerk? His dad had it coming. Everything he'd said and more. Mike didn't have the right to pull the father card.

He wished... He wanted...

Nick sighed. It didn't make any difference what he wanted. No one cared anyway. He sighed again, bent down, and began picking up the dirty clothes. Grabbing the polka-dot boxers, his face flushed. He flung the shorts into the laundry basket and quickly covered them with a dirty t-shirt before wandering out into the hall.

The house felt empty, but he hadn't heard his dad leave, so he was around somewhere. Nick found him sitting on an overstuffed sofa in the family room. The glass walls of the room, which stretched the entire width of the house, show-cased an intricately landscaped in-ground pool in the back-yard and in the distance, a row of mountains that stretched across the western horizon. Nick had already discovered the room was his dad's favorite place to relax. But as he watched from the kitchen, he could see that Mike was far from relaxed. Perched stiffly on the edge of the sofa, his dad stared out the windows, but Nick was pretty sure he wasn't enjoying the view.

Feeling like an intruder, Nick backed up, intending to return to his room. As he did, he bumped a barstool causing it to screech like the chairs in the Fountain Creek visitors lounge. Mike startled as if he had just awakened and looked over at him. He didn't appear angry any more. He looked exactly like what Nick had called him — a failure.

"Nick, come and sit down. Please." It was almost a ques-tion, certainly not a command.

He ambled over and dropped onto the far end of the sofa. "Nice," he finally said about the view, just to break the uncomfortable silence.

"What?"

He wasn't sure if his dad hadn't heard him or if he was asking something else, so he sat there, silently waiting and wishing he was just about anywhere else.

Mike finally turned and looked at him with a puzzled expression. "What's nice?"

With a shrug of indifference, Nick nodded towards the snow-capped mountains. "We don't have those in Chicago." Without planning to, he heard himself say, "Is that why you moved out here? The mountains, the skiing, or something?"

"No." Slowly, Mike seemed to draw back into the room. "I was born in a small town just a few miles south of here. Your grandparents lived there after they moved here from León, Mexico."

Nick had never even wondered where his dad had been born. It was kind of weird thinking about Mike as a kid, let alone a baby. "So how'd you end up in Chicago?" He was surprised that he was actually curious. "Seems weird."

Mike gave him a weary, lopsided smile. "I suppose it does, but to your mom and me, it was an adventure. Neither of us had ever lived outside of Colorado, so when I got accepted in the graduate program in Chicago, we jumped on it. Your mom got a job, and I was busy at the university. Then you were born." He hesitated before adding, "It was a good time."

Nick tried to envision a time he couldn't remember. A time when his parents had been young and happy and maybe even in love. "So what happened?" he said, not sure he really wanted to know.

Mike gave him an awkward shrug. "Things happen. First, I got an offer to teach at the University in Denver, and eventually, I took the job here." The job Mike referred to so casually was that of a full professor and head of the Sciences Department at the local branch of the University. Mike didn't talk much about his job, but Nick knew from things his mom and Jo had said that not only did his dad make good money, he was well-respected and a sought-after speaker and writer.

"And, your grandmother was here. She needed someone to look after her," Mike continued. "With my father out of the picture, there wasn't anyone else. As for your mom...well, she had her own career. I didn't blame her for not wanting to leave Chicago to start over in Colorado." They sat silently for a few moments, deep within their own thoughts. "But, there's a lot to be said for Colorado Springs," Mike added and nodded towards the span of windows overlooking the mountains. "Not the least of which is the view."

Not knowing what to say to his dad's revelations, Nick reached in his pocket and pulled out the coin. He ran his finger over the rows of raised symbols. There seemed to be two parts, almost like a coin inside a coin, but he couldn't figure out how they were attached. Nick twisted the two parts. They moved in opposite directions, the outer part clockwise, the inner counterclockwise. He lined up the tiny markings, experimenting to see if he could find a pattern.

The soft clicking caught Mike's attention. "What do you have there?"

Nick hesitantly handed over the coin. Mike pulled out his glasses and studied it with interest, holding it so close the coin almost touched his nose. Grasping it carefully by the edge, he lifted it, allowing the light to reflect off the dull surface.

"'Pontis Viator,'" Mike read. "That's Latin for…. Let me think for a minute." He hesitated only slightly. "Bridge Traveler."

Nick looked at Mike with disbelief. "You're joking, right? You can read Latin?"

Mike shrugged, looking uncomfortable at the attention. "A little here and there. You pick up things at the University."

"So, what's that mean? Bridge Traveler?"

Mike shook his head. "I have no idea." They both stared at the coin for a moment before Mike flipped it back to Nick. "Where'd you get it?"

He thought of Miriam. 'There is a Watcher always.' The way she'd said it, a Watcher had to be a person or a being of some kind. The whole thing was too bazaar, and the idea of someone or something always watching him creeped him out.

There was no way he was going to tell his dad about the strange encounter in the break room. Besides, he wasn't sure what he thought about Miriam and her cryptic words. He needed time to process the meeting before he shared it with anyone, least of all Mike. He didn't trust him. Who knew what Mike might pull? Maybe some crazy parent thing like over-reacting, calling the police, and having the crazy red-head arrested. Nick didn't want her arrested. He wanted to find her and get some information from her. He stared down at the coin, trying to come up with a convincing lie.

Before that happened, Mike interrupted. "Listen, about earlier. I didn't mean…"

Nick shrugged, refusing to make eye contact. He didn't want to hear some lame excuse, or worse, some gushy apology. It was so much easier keeping Mike at arm's length. He frowned, tilting his head. "What's that noise?"

Mike seemed almost grateful for the interruption. "What noise? I don't hear anything."

Nick massaged his ears. It reminded him of the cabin pressure change in an airplane, or being underwater in a pool. "You can't hear that buzzing?" He yawned and shook his head, trying to clear the uncomfortable feeling.

"Buzzing?" Mike looked concerned. "Bud Leonard's mowing his lawn down the street. Maybe that's what you're hearing."

Nick frowned as the pressure built, making his eardrums pound. "It's not some stupid mower. It sounds like," he hesitated then stopped, listening. It wasn't so much a buzzing as a hissing or spitting. Like a horde of people had surrounded the house holding sparklers or live electrical wires.

The thought made him nervous, and he shot an uneasy glance at the windows. Absently, he scratched at his arms. Only then did he notice that he felt like something was crawling on him. He wiggled, scratching his back on the couch cushion, trying to get rid of the uncomfortable feeling.

"Maybe you need some water or something," Mike suggested uncertainly.

Nick just shook his head. He got up and moved over to the windows. Craning his neck, he tried to see if the yard had been invaded. "There's nothing out there, but it's getting louder. I don't get it." He glanced back at Mike who had stood up. "You really don't hear that?"

"Are you sure you don't need some water?" Mike shifted his weight from one foot to the other; he looked lost. "I know! How about tea? I think Rosa made some."

"I don't want anything to drink!" Nick shouted. The hissing and spitting intensified until Nick thought the windows would shatter. His whole body itched as if something alive was crawling under his skin. He pressed the palms of his hands to his ears.

This was it. He was going crazy. He wondered if Grandma Carlota had felt this way when she'd started going nuts.

Suddenly, there was a new sound, a throbbing heartbeat that made him cringe and at the same time called to him like something familiar. Something he'd known but had forgotten. Maybe it was the Watcher's heartbeat. The thought frightened him. Caught like a leaf in a current, Nick felt himself hold up the coin and stare at it owlishly. As if from a distance, he heard himself say, "It's warm."

"What is?" Mike cleared his throat. Clutching his cell phone as if he were trying to decide whether to call an ambulance or a priest, or maybe Rosa, he stepped close to Nick.

"The coin. It's getting warmer."

"No." Mike shook his head. "That's not possible. It's probably just the alloy conducting heat because of your core body temperature."

Nick glared at him. "Yeah, Professor. Well, my core temperature is rising then because this thing is getting hot." Although common sense said to get rid of it, Nick clutched the coin like a lifeline. He stared transfixed as the coin's center suddenly pulsed crimson in time with his own heartbeat. His eyes widened; his breathing shallowed. Then, just because something told him he should, he mumbled, "Sic, Dominus."

He looked at Mike, and with his free hand grabbed his dad's sleeve. "I-I think it's time to go," Nick said, but he didn't know why.

CHAPTER 3

CRIMP TOWN

Nick had watched tons of science fiction. Any true sci-fi fan could describe in vivid detail the spinning, whirling, "washing machine in a spin cycle" special effects of some poor soul being sucked down a tunnel that everyone knew was going to end up in a really, really bad place. The screams and wails of the unfortunate victim, accompanied by the buzzing, crackling, sucking sounds of a massive vortex, were as familiar to Nick as his own heartbeat.

This was nothing like that.

Not even close.

This was being sucked into a bubble. This was no time. No space. This was being surrounded by a vacuum of silence. Held in suspense, unmoving.

One second Nick was hearing the sound of his own voice telling Mike it was time to go and the next it was nothing. Absolutely nothing.

He couldn't feel his own skin. He couldn't hear his heartbeat or even tell whether he was breathing. He was contained in a silence more absolute than anything he could have imagined; he was wrapped in a nonexistence that defied words and logic. He couldn't tell if he was standing or sitting or suspended in space. He couldn't see the landscaped pool or the mountains or Mike or even himself. He saw nothing but a warm light that fluttered against a background of soft blue. It was like lying on his bed in his sunlit room while Rosa snapped a clean blue sheet into the air above his head, the soft, cool cotton falling all over him like a mountain breeze.

Nick wanted to cry. It was the sweetest, purest peace he'd ever known. He forgot he missed his mom, Chicago, his friends. He forgot he was mad. He forgot that he was just a kid who hated his dad and the world. There was nothing but this place that wasn't a place.

Then there was chaos.

"Get yer gummy hands off me!" It was a woman's voice, strident, more angry than scared.

"Curse you back" a man yelled.

Somewhere far away, a dog barked, a child shrieked, and a train whistled.

Overhead, sea gulls clamored.

Someone else, a male voice, called, "C'mon back. C'mon back."

"Here you be then," a woman's voice murmured in his ear, causing Nick to let go of Mike's sleeve and spin around.

He was standing in a narrow, dirty alleyway, the coin clutched in his hand like a talisman. They were alone, except for a woman in a long skirt stepping out of sight around the corner of a nearby building.

Nick shoved the coin into a pocket of his jeans and looked around, wondering what had just happened.

On one side were wooden buildings all slightly canted towards them as if eavesdropping. On the other were similar buildings listing away from them, perhaps afraid of hearing what might be said. The effect threw Nick off balance. He shifted his feet to steady himself, raising a cloud of dust.

He looked up to a blue sky just like the one over Colorado Springs: staggered shades of blue streaked with wispy, white clouds. The brilliant sun beamed down as hot and heavy as an iron. Except for the gulls, which had no place in a Colorado sky, it all looked normal. But Nick knew with certainty that he was in an alien place.

He also knew he should be feeling fear, anxiety, anticipation, confusion. But instead of any of those, he felt only disappointment and homesickness. They were the same emotions that had colored his days these last five weeks, but the feelings now were more vivid, more gut-wrenching. They were real.

And it was all because of the bubble. He knew it. Everything paled in comparison to the peace that existed there. Everything: his feelings these last several weeks, his family, his friends, and even the fact that he was no longer in Colorado. Maybe not even on Earth.

"Pike's Peak," Mike said.

Nick flinched, not so much because of the ordinariness of Mike's voice, but because the lingering effects of the recent sci-fi experience snapped off like a light. He frowned at his dad. "What?"

Mike turned in a slow circle, scanning their surroundings as Nick had just done. "No Pike's Peak." He glanced down at the cell phone still in his hand then shot a wide-eyed look at Nick. "No signal," Mike said, in a voice suddenly filled with consternation.

That really was scary! Nick felt his mouth go dry. "What the heck is going on?"

"This can't be," Mike mumbled.

"What?"

"No." Mike shook his head slowly.

Feeling younger than he had in a long time, Nick reached out to clutch at his dad's sleeve again. He stopped short, forcing his clenched fists to drop to his sides. "What can't be?" Mike's eyes teared up. That scared Nick more than anything that had happened to him ever. Scarier even than finding out you were being sent far away to live with a virtual stranger. His fists tightened. "What can't be?" he repeated.

Mike looked Nick's way, staring through him. "She was right." Then he blinked and his dark eyes came into focus. "My father. Impossible as it seems, I think…I think my mother was right about him," Mike slowly admitted.

Nick frowned and brushed the hair from his eyes in order to stare up at his dad. "The folding space thing?" Mike simply nodded. "But how did—" Nick gasped and shoved his hand back in his pocket, pulling out the coin. "Miriam."

"Who?"

"I met a lady. Earlier. At Fountain Creek. She said she knew you and Grandpa. She's the one who gave me the coin. The one that says Bridge Traveler." Nick held out the coin, but Mike just looked at it without touching it. "Miriam called me a Traveler."

Mike flinched as if he'd been hit in the face.

"What?" Nick said, slipping the coin back in his pocket for safekeeping.

"And she called herself Miriam. You're sure?"

"Yeah." There was something his dad wasn't telling him. He wasn't sure he wanted to know what it was, but he asked anyway. "Why?"

"Nicco, I think we need to talk. I—"

"Ay! You two!" A man wearing baggy brown pants, short boots, and a filthy, oversized shirt stood at the end of the alley. He pointed at them with an even filthier hand.

It might not be Chicago, but Nick recognized the threat in the man's voice and stance. So, he did exactly what he would have done back in the Windy City. He ordered, "Run!" and took off in the opposite direction, assuming that Mike would follow.

"Nicco?"

Nick wanted to tell his dad to quit calling him that, but he was a little busy at the moment. He was pretty sure his sneakers were raising a cloud of alien dust. Then again, based on the sounds coming from behind him, Mike was raising a dust cloud of his own. The sounds of their shoes slapping the hard-packed dirt and their heavy breathing nearly drowned out the "Blimy grubbers!" curse that emanated from the stranger at the other end of the alley.

A hand grabbed his right shoulder, stopping him mid-stride. Before he could fight back, he realized it was his dad. "This way," Mike instructed as he tugged Nick behind him into a narrow passageway between two buildings. It was the same place that the woman had disappeared into a few moments earlier.

Nick stumbled along in Mike's wake. The only light was a meager shaft of sun wedged between the overhanging roofs of the buildings and a narrow band of brightness ahead where the alleyway ended. They were both breathing hard, and he was stepping on things that he couldn't see. When something moved beneath his shoe, he lunged forward, bumping into Mike.

"Sorry," he grunted.

Mike slowed, keeping Nick behind him with his arm. "Why did you run?"

"What?"

Mike stopped and looked at him. "What made you run?"

"You're kidding, right?" When Mike just shrugged, Nick realized that his dad the professor was totally clueless. "You didn't see that guy back there? The greasy one with the weird clothes and the nasty look on his face?"

"Well, yeah. But I thought maybe he just...I don't know. Maybe we were trespassing and he just wanted to warn us."

"Uh-huh," Nick mumbled doubtfully.

"You shouldn't be so distrustful of people, Nick. Not everyone's out to get you, you know."

"Sure. That's a good topic for discussion some other time when we're not, well...here." Mike frowned at Nick's condescending tone, but before his dad could comment further, Nick changed the subject. "So, other than in a dark alley, where are we? What happened? What made you say Grandma was right?"

Mike sighed and took a deep breath before leaning back against the wall of the nearest building. He looked back the way they'd come as he spoke. "I don't know. This is unbelievable, and yet," he lifted a hand, "here we are."

"So, Grandma was right, which means that your dad didn't run out on you. Right?"

Looking wounded, Mike stared into the space over Nick's head. "I don't know. It's just," he hesitated then shook his head. "It's like a dream from a long time ago. I remember fragments of it. I was your age, maybe younger. A woman with red hair. Watching me. Always watching me."

"What happened?"

Mike chewed his lower lip. "I-I told her to go away and leave me alone. I told her no." His forehead puckered as he stared into Nick's eyes. "I would swear her name was Miriam, but it couldn't be. It was a dream. Wasn't it, Nicco? I mean, if it had really happened, why would I have forgotten that until now? After all these years? What does it mean?"

Nick felt sorry for the man in front of him. "It means your dad could be out there somewhere. He could even be here."

Mike's eyes flashed then he pulled himself away from the wall, his six foot frame towering over Nick. "Then I intend to find out," he said, and turning, he strode up the alleyway.

Hurrying to catch up, Nick studied his dad's dark silhouette. His back was straight, his hands were curled into loose fists, and his long legs ate up the dirt alleyway with purpose. He looked like someone bent on vengeance, and perhaps he was. Nick could definitely picture the man in front of him in charge of a whole college department, and he pitied the college student who dared talk back to him.

Nick's insides fluttered just like the first time he'd ridden the Raging Bull at Six Flags. But this thrill wasn't from fear, even though it probably should have been considering they had no idea what had just happened or where they were. Instead, this thrill felt strangely like pride — pride that the tall stranger in front of him was his dad.

Before he had time to consider the feeling further, however, it was gone. Vanished. Knocked out of him when that long, rigid spine slammed into his face as Mike came to a dead stop at the end of the alley. His face pressed into his dad's back, Nick froze for a second and then, for the first time since he'd been a little kid, he leaned against his dad. A vague, once-familiar sense of security struggled to rear its head, awakened by the nearness of the man in front of him.

"Holy cow," Mike mumbled, dispelling the moment.

Pulling away, Nick stepped around his dad to look at what had brought him to such a sudden halt. All he could manage was, "Uh...yeah."

It looked like they'd stepped onto a movie set. Maybe a western sci-fi, with lots of horses, clapboard buildings, wagons, filthy kids chasing scrawny dogs, and humans in every shape and size dressed in grungy, heavy-looking clothes. Nick wouldn't have been surprised to see someone dressed in a rubber alien suit walk out of the nearest store.

He sniffed. Water. A whole lot of water. He recognized the smell from living near Lake Michigan his whole life. And over the sounds of the animals and the gulls and the people, he heard waves. They had to be near a large body of water.

The street was lined on each side with two-story buildings fronted by small windows and wooden sidewalks. To their left, a woman stepped down from the sidewalk and crossed in front of them. She gave them a surreptitious glance as she walked by, her eyes lingering on Nick's mouth. Her hair was tangled, and she smelled like she hadn't bathed in weeks. She stepped onto the sidewalk to their right, continuing down the street without slowing.

Without thinking, Nick reached up, slipped off his lip ring, and tucked it into his pocket with the coin.

"This is crazy." Mike looked around them then glanced down at Nick. "This is crazy, right?"

"Way."

"I don't believe this," Mike murmured. Then, "Come on." He stepped onto the sidewalk and started down the street.

"Where are we going?"

"I don't know. We need to find someone who can tell us what's going on."

"Uh, Mike." Nick stopped and pointed to a gap between two buildings across the street. Water was visible, but not just a pond or a river or even a lake. An ocean stretched into infinity.

"That's impossible."

Nick wanted to laugh. His dad thought an ocean was impossible? What about the fact that one second they were standing in their family room in Colorado Springs facing a mountain range and the next they were standing in the old west?

Mike stopped when an elderly couple stepped out of a doorway and crossed the sidewalk right in front of them. The man was carrying what might have been a bag of flour and the old woman was cradling a ham.

"A store," Nick said.

"Yeah. Maybe we should check in there. Surely, there's someone who can tell us something."

"Like what?"

Mike stared down at him. "Well, like where we are."

"If you say so."

"What's wrong?"

Nick shrugged. "I don't see how that's going to help us."

"Nicco, did you stop to think they might be able to tell us how we got here?"

"I know how we got here." 'And my name isn't Nicco,' he silently added, even though it didn't seem that important at the moment.

Mike frowned. "Well, it can't hurt to ask. When you have a problem, the first order of finding a solution is to gather information." He glanced at the doorway through which the old couple had emerged. "Wait here. I'll be right back."

Nick watched Mike disappear inside the building. "This isn't some stupid word problem from a math book," he muttered as he leaned up against a post supporting the porch roof to wait. Above his head, a piece of paper fluttered in an ocean-laden breeze. He turned to stare up at the fancy script on the handwritten note.

"From the Keeper of the Third Bridge with respect to the Gathering of the Shades," he read softly.

"Do not be doing that," someone ordered.

Standing two steps below him on the dirty street stood a dark-haired boy. He looked at least a couple of years younger than Nick. Then again, it could have been an illusion created by the fact that he was unwashed and underfed. Wavy hair fell in long, uncombed locks around his smudged face, contrasting sharply with large eyes that were the same weak, washed-out blue as the sky. Like every other male Nick had seen here, the boy wore an oversized shirt and woolen pants. But unlike the others, this boy also had what looked like a crusty blanket tied around his neck and the pockets of his pants were bulging. Nick got the distinct impression that the boy was wearing everything he owned.

"Do not be doing what?"

The boy pointed at the post with his chin. "We do not be speaking of the Gathering. At least, not in public."

"Why? What is it?"

The boy's eyes widened. "You truly be not from Tempest."

So, this place was called Tempest, Nick thought as he looked down at himself. "What gave me away? My clothes, or the fact that I wear deodorant?"

The boy scowled. "Yer companion, he be going in there, did he not?" he said, glancing at the store.

"Yeah. So?"

"Then we haven't much time. Follow me." The boy headed for a narrow gap between the store and the next building.

"Excuse me?" Nick had no intention of going anywhere without Mike and he especially wasn't going to take orders from some homeless kid.

"Do you be wanting to save him or not?"

It was Nick's turn to scowl. "Save him from what? He just went in to ask directions."

The boy glanced around as if making sure no one was listening. "The owner be a known crimp." When Nick didn't respond, he sighed. "It may be too late already. They be sneaking out through the back, they will. Come on." And with that, he slipped into the crevice.

Against his better judgment and unsure of why he was doing it, Nick followed. Before squeezing himself into the tiny crack, he took a last look around. Sometime during his conversation with the kid, the street had cleared, like it did before the big gunfight scene in a western movie. The only person in sight was a woman staring at him from behind a grimy window in the building across the street. She shook her head slowly, sadly. Even as he crept through the dark gap, Nick was haunted by the sadness and familiarity surrounding the strange woman.

"Here," the boy whispered. He had stopped, and kneeling in the dirt, he looked out onto the alleyway behind the store.

Peering over his shoulder, Nick could see two men. One was wearing a long apron over his clothes. The other was dressed in dark blue flannel pants and a dingy white shirt.

The man in the apron wrote something on a piece of paper and handed it to the man in blue. "And mind you don't be forgetting. I keep my own account, you know."

"Aye. You be a regular now, ain't you? So why would I be forgetting?" the blue-clad man grumped. "Bring him on," he said and waved to someone out of Nick's view.

He heard a scuffling sound then three men exited the back of the store. Two were dressed identically in gray flannel pants and shirts. The third was...

"No!"

Nick clambered over the boy in front of him in an effort to get to his dad, but the boy's filthy hands clamped onto his arm, holding him back. Mike turned at the sound of Nick's yell. His mouth was gagged and blood dripped down the left side of his face. He shook his head vehemently, grunting and fighting against the two men who held him.

The man in blue nodded to the men struggling to hold Mike. "On with you. Or do you need another tap of my stick alongside your head?" As the two men dragged Mike down the alley, the man folded the paper, shoved it into a pocket on his shirt, and glanced over at Nick. "Who be you?"

"What are you doing? Where are you taking him?"

"No," the boy holding him hissed as he tightened his hold on Nick and tried to tug him deeper into the gap between the buildings.

The man in the apron approached. "Would you be with the stranger then, lad?"

Keeping his eye on Mike and struggling to free himself from the boy's grip, Nick barely registered the man's question.

"I said, be you with him?"

As Mike and the two men disappeared around a corner, Nick looked up at the man. His face bore the same look of hate and lust and greed as the man who'd spied them in the alleyway earlier.

"He's—he's..."

"He's with me," the boy said.

Nick looked at the boy then at the man. His heart felt like it was going to burst out of his chest and his raging pulse hammered against the backs of his eyes. He didn't know what to do. He was scared. He wanted to find Mike. But he didn't want to be beaten up and dragged off.

"Well?" the man barked, his hand hovering over the thick wooden club shoved in his belt.

The boy stared up at him, and like the woman in the window, he slowly shook his head.

Nick swallowed. His mouth was dry. He opened it. "I'm with him," he mumbled and nodded his head towards the young boy. "I—I don't know that man," he said, and he wanted to cry.

CHAPTER 4

WHO BE THE TOUGHEST OF THEM ALL

There was a rough tug on the tail of Nick's t-shirt. Out of the corner of his eye, he saw the scrawny boy edging away, his dirty clothing melding into the gloom of the alley. "I've gotta go," Nick muttered to the aproned man, retreating a step.

"Half a minute, lad. We be needing to chat." A meaty hand clamped down on his shoulder, but Nick twisted sideways and stumbled backwards. The dirty fingernails digging into his skin lost their hold. "Curse you for a Tempest wharf rat!"

The oath proved all the motivation Nick needed to bolt.

For the next five minutes, Nick concentrated on nothing but putting distance between himself and the irate man. Raw fear colored his survival instinct. He ran faster than he had ever run in his life. That was a good thing, because the boy in front of him was quick and seemed sure of his way even though they were racing through a maze of dark alleys and dusty side streets. Nick glanced around as he ran, trying to spy landmarks, but in the gloom of the surrounding buildings, every turn looked the same. He finally gave up and simply focused on not allowing the boy, darting through the shadows like a rat, to give him the slip.

And then, without warning, the boy vanished, leaving Nick alone and winded. He skidded to a stop. Gasping for air, he bent over trying to catch his breath. The shadows grew, looming over him, threatening to pounce. Hesitantly, he took a step forward then choked off a yelp when he slipped in a puddle of something that smelled like cat pee. He struggled to keep from falling on his butt.

Recovering his balance, he looked around him. "Kid?" he panted softly. "Where'd you go?"

He jumped when a shadow on his right hissed, "This way."

Stepping towards the sound, Nick squinted until he could make out a smudged face peering up at him through a jagged hole in a board fence that looked perilously close to collapse.

"Come," the boy whispered. "We be here."

"Great," Nick muttered sarcastically, "we be wherever here is." Heaving a disgusted sigh, he dropped to his knees and squirmed through the hole.

Struggling out the other side, he found himself standing in a small courtyard surrounded on one side by the wobbly fence and on the other three sides by crumbling brick buildings. The windowless structures cast a dark cloud of claustrophobia bordered by a hedgerow of profound darkness, a product of both the shadows and the sad nature of the place. The sagging edifices dominated the scene like age-old sentries, blind and dying. Nick had to admit the courtyard made a great, albeit dismal, hideout that he never would have found on his own.

Under a strong impression that he was being watched by more than just the stone guardians and the skinny kid, Nick took a few steps toward the center of the courtyard. His skin crawled at the loud crunching sound that came with each step, but there was nothing he could do about it. The ground was covered by a thick layer of litter.

A quick perusal revealed that a lot of the rubbish had probably been scrounged and purposely brought here for some unknown reason. "Great," he mumbled, "I'm hiding in the city dump."

He glanced over at his underfed guide. Standing in his baggy cocoon of ill-fitting clothes, the boy reeked of frailty. There was no way he was strong enough to man-handle some of the garbage Nick saw, like the huge, rusty ship's bell laying on its side. Just as Nick wondered why someone would go to all the trouble to haul it here, he spotted a pile of rags folded inside the bell's cavernous mouth — a shelter and a bed for someone.

He wrinkled his nose against the sour odor punching him in the face. "Home sweat home," he grunted, breathing through his mouth. With effort, he feigned a relaxed stance, tossed his long hair out of his eyes, and casually bent down to dust off his jeans.

The boy eyed him like a stray dog waiting for scraps, but Nick purposefully ignored him. With a confident sneer as fake as the lip ring tucked in his pocket, he crossed his arms and scanned the courtyard as his eyes grew accustomed to the gloom. Within moments, he spotted several hunched forms sitting in silent, ragged clusters in the deep shadows of the buildings. More underfed kids like the one standing beside him. As one, they stared at him then, apparently considering him no threat, they returned to what they'd been doing.

One group was taking turns tossing a stone as close as possible to a line drawn in the dirt. Soft, mingled taunts and curses, combined with the clinking of coins, told Nick that the outcome of the game involved more than just being labeled the winner.

A boy in another group moved, revealing a small fire. Nick inched closer to them and watched as a kid of indeterminate age and sex stirred a gooey mixture that looked like dirty oatmeal in a dented pot. A cloud of tiny insects buzzed, occasionally landing on the bubbling glop. Nick's stomach churned in protest and his lip curled in disgust. As he watched, the biggest figure in the group backhanded a smaller boy, knocking him to the ground amidst raucous laughter.

Nick's escort stepped in front of him and reached to grasp his hand. "Welcome." The boy frowned, clearly confused when Nick jerked his hand away.

"Sorry, man." Embarrassed that he might have betrayed how nervous he really was, Nick lied, "It's just, I'm not into touching. And, no offense, but you're kind of a germaphobe's worst nightmare."

The boy's frown deepened. He glanced at his hand, wiped it on the front of his coat, and stuck it in his pocket. "I be Simon, son of Laban."

"Nick, son of...." He shot another quick glance at his surroundings. Everything in him was telling him to run, but he couldn't, at least not until he found out what had happened to Mike. And right now, Simon, son of Laban, was his only lead. He cleared his throat. "So, what happened back there? Where'd they take Mike, the guy I was with?"

Simon shifted his weight from foot to foot. "Be you hungry? Fresh burgoo be on the fire." He licked his lips, looking with hungry eyes towards the bubbling pot.

Nick's stomach heaved at the very thought. "Thanks, but I'll pass. I asked about Mike. What happened to him?" Nick insisted.

Simon shrugged. "He be going into the store of a crimp," he offered, his eyes shifting between Nick and the pot of grungy oatmeal.

Nick scowled. "Okay, so that's as clear as your porridge over there." He waited impatiently, but when Simon remained mute, he snapped, "What the heck is a crimp? Can you at least tell me that much?"

Simon chewed his dirty thumbnail, studying Nick with his pale blue eyes. Finally, tucking his hand back in his pocket, he said, "A crimp be...he just be a crimp. What else would he be?"

"I shouldn't have come here," Nick muttered darkly. "It was a mistake. This is crazy. I should have stayed back there and tried to help." He tried not to think about the fact that he'd denied knowing his dad.

"Help?" Simon said.

Nick didn't bother to hide his contempt for the other boy. "Is this too complicated for you? You just don't get it, do you? That guy those big dudes were dragging away? His name is Mike, and," he swallowed hard and added softly, "he's my dad." At Simon's puzzled look, he clarified. "He's my father. I need to find him, so we can get out of here. He was hurt, bleeding."

"He be alive."

For a second, Nick wasn't sure it was Simon who had mumbled the simple words of hope. The boy was staring at his feet with the intensity of someone revealing a well-guarded secret. "How do you know?" Nick demanded. He wanted to shake the kid like a piggy bank until the answers spilled out.

"It be the way it always be. Only the faces and those they leave behind change," Simon whispered as he scuffed the toe of his crude leather moccasin through a layer of litter. "Why be it different this time?"

Nick released an impatient sigh. "I don't suppose you know where they took him?"

Simon shrugged and looked away.

"I've got to get out of this dump." Nick turned, seeking escape back through the hole in the fence, when a voice stopped him.

"This stranger be insulting our home, Simon." A tall, muscular boy stepped out of the shadows between Nick and the fence. He was much older than Simon, older even than Nick, and he stared unblinking at Nick's face. Despite his shabby clothes, he was draped in authority much like Simon was draped in his disgusting blanket. Fighting intimidation, Nick pulled himself up to his full height, crossed his arms, and cocked his head, hoping he looked calm and unconcerned.

"He did not be meaning it, Elliard," Simon said, his voice intense, but deferential. "He be one of the not knowing."

"Knowing what?" Nick croaked, his mouth as dry as dust. His eyes darted between the two boys, looking for a clue.

Contemplating Nick like a predator searching out wounded prey, the one called Elliard reached into his shirt pocket, casually pulled out a sliver of bone, and began to pick his teeth. His hostile eyes never left Nick's as he declared in a harsh voice, "Simon, son of Laban, you be bringing this surf slug into the Sanctuary. The rules be simple." The cold eyes shifted to glare at Simon. "Is it a refresher you be needing?"

Simon's face paled beneath his dirt mask. Eyes downcast, he murmured, "No, Elliard, please. I be knowing the rules all right. I do."

Elliard snorted derisively then looked at Nick once more. "Why you be here, boy?" His eyes raked down Nick's clothes and landed hungrily on his expensive tennis shoes. Nick followed the boy's gaze, looking at his own feet as if seeing them for the first time. Fighting not to squirm, Nick watched the dark eyes drift slowly upward until oozing hostility locked onto his face with such intensity that it felt like he'd been grabbed. "Sanctuary be not for the likes of you," Elliard announced.

Nick's attention was focused on the boy in front of him, but he was also vaguely aware of other forms drifting out from the shadows to surround them. A shudder sprinted down his spine as Elliard studied him, measured him, and by the sneer that formed on his face, apparently found him lacking.

"Speak," Elliard commanded him.

But it was Simon who piped, "His father be gathered by the crimp."

"Let him answer," Elliard ordered. Simon's eyes darted to Nick's face, silently warning him of the dangers that lay in a wrong response.

Nick uncrossed his arms, rubbed his sweaty palms on his jeans, and licked his dry lips. As if he needed Simon's mute warning. After all, he was streetwise, and everything in him screamed, 'Retreat!' But there was no place to go, no escape. Gang members continued to emerge from the shadows like feral dogs, boxing him in, tightening the chokehold of fear that was already suffocating him.

He shifted his stance and squinted at Elliard through his long hair. "Some men, Simon called them crimps, took my dad."

"He be not taken by the crimp." Elliard betrayed no emotion. "He be sold."

Nick wasn't sure which was more unnerving, Elliard's flat words or the detached gaze of his hooded eyes. "How do I get him back?" he choked out.

"Be you stupid?" Elliard snapped. "He be gone. Sold to a Shade Runner."

A voice from the circle surrounding them droned, "A Shade Runner from Tempest to Bridge End." There were grunts of affirmation.

"Sell this one, too," another voice growled.

"Hey, man," Nick held up his hands in a non-threatening gesture, "thanks for the hospitality. You've been a big help, but I'm going to take off now."

A gravelly voice chimed in, "Aye, he be a Traveler maybe. A stranger for sure. Sell 'em, El."

"Sell 'em!" The threats were bolder now, coming in a volley, like stones being slung from all directions. Nick felt the tension growing, but he didn't know how to defuse it.

"Enough!" Elliard shouted. "That be my decision alone." The attack stopped immediately, and Elliard gave a grim, self-assured smile. "We be having fresh meat for the pot, thanks to Simon's quick thinking," he said as he turned away.

Nick allowed a shallow breath to escape through clenched teeth. The sense of relief he felt was overwhelming, and short-lived.

"Hold him while Jaska be helping him empty them pockets," Elliard muttered.

Before Nick could react, two of the larger boys had grabbed his arms, pinning them to his sides, while a third threw an arm around his neck from behind. Wriggling and twisting, Nick tried to no avail to keep a small kid, obviously named Jaska, from rifling his pockets with grubby fingers.

"Get your hands off me!" he gasped as the arm around his neck tightened. Kicking out, Nick managed to send a glancing blow off Jaska's cheek, sending him backwards on his skinny behind. It was a fleeting victory that ended when the boy scrambled to his feet with a curse.

"Hold them feet," Elliard ordered and two more boys pinned Nick's legs.

Prying fingers wrapped around Miriam's coin and pulled it from Nick's pocket along with a half-dozen coins he had left from the vending machine, a paper clip, the lip ring, and his student ID. There was a triumphant yell and Jaska's eyes lit up, reflecting the dim glow of a sun that had lowered behind the building to his left. "Elliard," Jaska shouted, "look what he be having!"

The leader's eyes widened as he took the bounty. Scratching at the laminated picture with a dirty fingernail, Elliard stared at Nick's likeness before dropping it onto the littered ground with a snort. The coins, the lip ring, and the paper clip disappeared as he thrust them deeply into his pocket. He met Simon's gaze with an enigmatic nod before turning back to Nick.

As Elliard stepped forward, Nick's captors released him and backed away. Before his brain could register his sudden freedom, Nick was shoved backwards. He stumbled, but with one flailing arm he managed to stop himself from hitting the ground. Struggling to regain his balance, he saw the gang shifting around him like a pack of wolves moving in for the kill. He staggered away from them until he literally had his back to the wall, his hands pressed against the deteriorating bricks of one of the ancient buildings. He frantically searched the eyes of the band of boys, looking for any sign of humanity. What he saw instead was feral apathy. His only possible ally, Simon, was nowhere to be seen. The ravenous wolves in front of him parted, allowing Elliard to swagger forward.

"This one would be making a fine meal for the lot of us, the whole of this month."

Did Elliard and the gang plan to eat him? Nick's heart raced as he recalled the bone toothpick he'd seen Elliard using. It was probably the last poor sap's little finger, and now that he thought about it, Elliard looked perfectly capable of cannibalism. He glanced around him. They all looked hungry enough to gnaw off their own arms, so why not someone else's? Nick gulped, cursing his own stupidity in blindly following Simon into this nightmare. He pressed himself against the crumbling bricks, fighting down bile that threatened to spew all over the gang leader's tattered moccasins.

Elliard moved in, shoving his face close to Nick's. "How much be you worth, boy?" he hissed. "Be you worth the price? Be there someone to redeem you?"

Breathing through his mouth as he tried to avoid the choking stench of Elliard's breath, Nick could hear the unmistakable sound of a knife being sharpened on a stone. Fear rose to meet the bile in his throat until he wasn't sure which he would gag on first. He shook his head. "I don't," he faltered, searching frantically for the right answer. "I don't know what you mean."

Anger honed the older boy's razor-sharp features. Nick flinched as Elliard grabbed the front of his shirt and slammed him hard against the wall. Once... Twice... Nick's head struck the bricks and the courtyard was jarred into a confusing jumble of flashes of light and streaks of dark.

"Do not be playing me for a fool, boy. I be master here. I be! One word from me and you be sold to the crimp, do you hear? Despite the Code of Honor. My reward would be great, and you would be following the path of the Shades. You be carrying coins." He slammed Nick against the bricks again followed by a stinging backhanded slap across the face. "You be carrying coins! Be there more hidden on your person? How be ye getting them? Be ye one of the Keeper's crimps, sent to weasel out our hidey hole?"

There were low grunts and unintelligible yelps of excitement from the semi-circle of spectators. Dazed, Nick knew he was out of options. His bruised thoughts raced, but only one stood out: He owed Mike an apology for denying that he knew him, and it probably wouldn't hurt to apologize to Jo, too, just for being a jerk. The level of his remorse caught Nick by surprise. There had been few times in his life that he'd felt the need to apologize to anyone for his actions. Stunned, he blinked back tears.

A second backhanded blow drove the tears and remorse away, and Nick could only lock his knees and focus on staying on his feet. If he slid to the ground, he knew his ribs would probably be Elliard's next target. He was pretty sure that even moccasin-clad feet could do some serious damage.

"I'm sorry," he gasped, struggling to find a way out. A way to stop the assault. "I don't," he stopped, sucking in a ragged breath. "Coins? You mean the change I had? It was nothing. Not even enough to buy a soda."

"You mock me, Stranger?"

Nick's eyes widened as the scarred knuckles of Elliard's fist suddenly filled his line of sight. Tendons stood out on the clenched hand, which was huge and unforgiving. Nick shut his eyes and shook his head, waiting mutely for pain to explode.

"Leave him be, Elliard!"

Nick thought he was imagining the voice. He waited for a long, tense moment before opening his eyes a slit. It was Simon. Standing next to his leader's tall frame, the ragged boy was dwarfed, but the knife he held poised to strike Elliard's stomach gave his words potency. With his grubby chin thrust out and his blue eyes as hard as ice, he certainly looked capable of murder.

"I be sticking you," Simon muttered. "You know it."

The tip of the blade inched forward, piercing tattered clothing and pricking skin. Elliard gasped and dropped his hands. "Is it traitor you be turning, Simon?" he asked in a low voice. "What be this one to you that you be willing to turn against yer own?"

Nick stood frozen. The only movement came from the cold beads of sweat slowly running down his neck and the twisting, turning dust motes that filled the twilight air. For the moment, Nick was a mere spectator, his eyes on the two shabby gladiators standing before him. Time passed slowly, but little Simon held his ground, refusing to back down from the leader who towered over him.

"Be it that way then?" Elliard finally said. "Redemption?" He cocked his head. "And what if redemption be only another of the Scribe's lore, Simon?" Seemingly ignoring the knife tip biting into his flesh, Elliard's eyes softened. "Does it mean so much that you would be taking such a chance?"

Simon's chin quivered as he responded with a single, quick nod. "It be me only chance. There be no other way."

Nick blinked and the knife was withdrawn. Another blink and it disappeared into a hidden pocket.

"Come, Nick," Simon ordered. "It be time to rest before we leave."

Dreamlike, Nick watched Simon stalk through the ring of silent boys, who only a moment before had been cheering for blood. Now, they shuffled out of Simon's way, creating an escape hatch.

Elliard took a step back and nodded to Nick, his eyes cutting towards Simon. "You be hearing him. Go."

Wiping stinging sweat from his eyes with a shaking hand, Nick stumbled after Simon, following the boy into the deep shadows of the buildings. Stepping around several piles of ragged blankets, Simon stopped. "We can be sleeping here. This spot be mine."

Nick glanced over his shoulder. "Are you nuts?" he hissed. "I can't stay here. What if that psycho changes his mind?"

Simon frowned. "If you be meaning Elliard, he will not come. Do you not understand? I be your protection." Whipping the blanket from around his neck, he tossed it to the ground, plopped down on it, and then stared up at Nick. "No harm be coming to you. I be seeing to that."

Nick studied the earnest face. He licked his lips, his tongue exploring a swollen cut and tasting blood. He must have bitten his lip when his brains were being bashed out against the wall. He gingerly felt the knot rising on the back of his head. For all his tough-guy persona, he'd never been in a real fight before, never been hit.

Looking towards the fence, he spied the jagged hole that led to the alley and back to where this nightmare had started. He wanted to leave, escape, and go find Mike. He wanted to be anywhere but here in this shadowy place filled with desperation and danger and the smell of unwashed bodies. Instinctively, he took a step towards the fence.

"It be not safe," Simon warned, his voice low and strained. "The patrols be out now. They be searching for strangers foolish enough to walk the streets of Tempest after dusk. Do not go, Nick. If they find you, they be taking you, too."

"Then maybe they'll take me to–"

"Listen!" Simon ordered, and cocked his head.

"What?" Nick heard nothing except the hushed sounds of homeless kids settling down for the night in a layer of filth, and perhaps, from a distance, the rush of winds carried ashore by the tide.

Simon's skin went even paler beneath its layer of dirt. "Shades. Do you hear? They be calling to one another across the waters."

"I don't understand," Nick said, anger edging his words. "You talk in riddles. Nothing you say makes sense. I'd be better off out there somewhere." He rubbed the back of his head and winced. "Anywhere, but here," he added and took another step in the direction of the alley.

Scrambling to his knees, Simon grabbed the hem of Nick's jeans with one hand and patted his soiled blanket with the other. "Please," he pleaded. "I be explaining. Besides, I have a gift." Reaching into his pocket, Simon pulled out the coins. Resting in the center of the dirty palm, Miriam's coin glimmered dully among the pennies, nickels, and dimes. "See."

Nick shook his head in disbelief. He hadn't really given the coin a thought since he and Mike had talked about it in the alley. But as he stared at the tiny raised symbols, he realized how desperately he needed it. "But, how?" he said. "Elliard took it."

Simon gave him a lopsided smile that showed a glimpse of decaying teeth. He patted the blanket again. Reluctantly, Nick dropped down beside him with a soft groan.

"I be lifting it," Simon whispered, glancing over his shoulder. "When Elliard be staring at my knife." He shrugged. "It wasn't hard. I could be teaching you, if you want. Then you be wanting for nothing. Tempest be full of fat merchants to pluck." Grinning, he dropped the coins in Nick's palm.

Nick stared at the foreign markings before squeezing his fist around the cool metal. The coin's edges dug into his flesh, making him feel safe despite his dire situation. Bowing his head, he closed his eyes and mumbled softly, "Thanks. I thought he was going to kill me."

"That be true," Simon offered nonchalantly. "Elliard has killed others."

Nick glanced around, embarrassed that Simon had witnessed the fear hiding behind his tough exterior. "Here, kid, thanks for your help." Clutching Miriam's coin tightly, he tossed the other coins into the dirt at his feet and watched with detachment as Simon scrambled for them.

The boy grinned and studied his treasure in a silent courtyard populated with hidden dangers. Nick could feel the threat. All around him. Lurking in the darkness.

"I've gotta get out of here," he whispered, hugging his knees tightly to his chest. "I've gotta go home." Clutching the coin, he thought of home, longed for the safety it offered — something he hadn't even known existed before he was dumped here. "Please," he begged, resting his forehead on his knees, "get me out of here. Sic, dominus. Please."

When he heard the buzzing, he raised his head. The pressure in his eardrums built. His skin was crawling, and his heart was pounding so hard that he looked to see if Simon could hear it. Tears filled his eyes as the coin's ruby center began to throb like a heartbeat, filling him with its warm promise. He shot a frantic glance at Simon. The last thing he saw before he was sucked into the bubble was Simon's face, drained of all color as the boy screamed, "No!"

93

CHAPTER 5

SPRINGING BACK

He sat alone on the floor of the family room, leaning against the sofa for support. Once again, the trip had left Nick emotionally drained. Empty. Wanting more. *Needing* more. So much more. More of something that he'd never known existed before today. Something that even now he couldn't name or identify.

As if awakening from a deep sleep, Nick sniffed, blinked, and looked around him. The same room that still didn't feel like home, with its smooth tile floor, plump sofa and matching chairs, heavy tables, polished lamps, and walls of glass. The room was just as they'd left it. Nothing had changed, except that instead of being the afternoon it was now night. The only light came from a moon peering over a mountain peak and the twinkle of nearby houses.

Nothing had changed, yet everything was different. Every single thing about his whole life had been altered. What he'd thought he'd known for a fact was wrong. What he'd thought was important suddenly seemed trivial. He thought about his friends back in Chicago and what they might be doing right now — riding the El, shoplifting a few beers, sneaking into a movie theater, maybe even smoking something they shouldn't, or at least talking about doing it. Just a few weeks ago, he'd have been right there with them, cheering them on. Now, it all seemed ignorant and juvenile. Nothing was the same.

Or was it? Maybe he'd dreamt it all. Maybe he was experiencing some sort of weird altitude sickness. Maybe it had never happened except in his head. He and Mike had never been transported to that other place. Mike hadn't been taken. Nick hadn't denied knowing him.

Mike was probably in his room right now, sleeping or reading one of those boring college papers he was always hauling around in his briefcase.

Using the couch for support, Nick pushed himself to his feet. He made his way into the kitchen on legs that trembled. The room smelled of the cleaner Rosa used on the sink and counters, and vaguely, of the banana peel Nick had tossed in the trash earlier in the day. The clock on the microwave glowed 9:38.

He stepped into the dining room. Feeling his way between the large buffet and a row of high-backed chairs, he made his way into the living room. Floor to ceiling glass outlined the door and angled a narrow beam of streetlight across the floor. The darkened fireplace on the north wall formed a menacing eye, the mantel a grim eyebrow, like a staring cyclops.

Nick shuddered. "Mike?" He meant to holler it out. Instead, his voice was soft and quavered like a shy school girl's. "Mike?" he said more loudly.

The only answer was an eerie silence and the sinister glare of the fireplace. Or maybe it wasn't an eye. Maybe it was a mouth, gaping wide, waiting for him to step close enough to—

A soft click from somewhere in the kitchen made Nick jerk. He stared back the way he'd come. Was there a shift in the shadows of the dining room? He didn't wait to find out. Not even bothering to feign bravery, he scurried past the maw of the fireplace and entered the dark hallway leading to the bedrooms.

Halfway down the long corridor, he wondered why he was walking around in the dark like a common burglar. Bumping against the framed photograph of the nearby Garden of the Gods that hung on the wall, Nick inched his way forward with his hand outstretched. His fingers brushed a wall switch and he flipped it. The light that flooded the hallway was harsh, and it plunged the living room behind him — and its lurking fireplace — into an abyss of dark obscurity.

Nick hurried to the door to Mike's room, opened it, and stared inside. "Mike?"

Nothing. No answer.

He entered the room. His glance took in the neatly made bed and the large walk-in closet before he stepped around the corner and entered the master bath. He flipped on the switch.

Standing across the room was a teenage boy with disheveled black hair and a dirty face.

Nick yelled.

So did the boy staring back at him.

Putting a hand over his thudding heart, he laughed nervously as he realized he was seeing his own image. Then he frowned and stepped closer to the mirror, examining his reflection. He lifted a hand to his left cheek, which was red and beginning to bruise. His lip was swollen where he'd bit it, and his wrinkled t-shirt bore grubby handprints on the shoulders and a small tear at the neck.

So, it hadn't been a dream after all. Elliard really had clipped him a good one on the face. Mike had been taken. Nick had denied knowing him.

Forgetting his trepidation about going through the dark, empty house, Nick ran from room to room hollering. For Mike, for Rosa, for Jo, for anyone. But there was no one. Just himself. He was alone.

Panting, he sank down beside the island in the kitchen and clutched the cordless telephone. His hands shook so badly that it took four tries before he hit the right combination of numbers. It rang five times before she answered, and when she did, it took him a few seconds to gather his voice.

"Mom?"

"Nicholas?" He heard sleep in her voice then a long pause filled with suspicion. "What's wrong now?"

"Dad's not here. There—"

"Nicholas..."

"—was a fight—"

"Nicholas..."

"—and I don't know how—"

"Nicholas!"

He stopped. "What?"

"There was a fight?" she said. Awake now, her voice was tight, barely controlled. Anger filled the connection like static. "Well?"

"Yes, but it wasn't–"

He was going to say it wasn't what she thought, it wasn't your typical teenage scuffle, but before he could finish, she snipped, "It never is. This is your dad's problem now. He can deal with it."

The phone went dead. He set it on the floor and stared at it. She'd said almost the exact same thing when she'd put him on the plane to Denver.

Nick scrubbed his eyes with his palms. He guessed he shouldn't blame her — not after all the trouble he'd caused her — but he did and it made him angry. Because this time, it really wasn't his fault. And this time, it wasn't his life at stake. It was Mike's. And although he might be a lousy father, Mike certainly hadn't done anything to deserve being dragged away and sold to a crimp. Whatever a crimp was.

So, Nick would have to figure out what to do on his own.

He could go back. Maybe. While he'd been sitting in the middle of the junky courtyard on Simon's filthy blanket, all he'd wanted was to get home. Now that he was here, safe, with no one threatening to kill him, the need to return gnawed at him.

But even assuming he could go back, what then?

He needed more information, but who knew anything about this? As far as he knew, there wasn't a book on strange coins that sent you flying through a bubble to an old west town. It wasn't like there was an expert he could turn to for advice on how to behave, how to rescue your dad from a crimp when he was lost in another dimension.

Or was there?

Nick frowned. Actually, there was one expert. Maybe even two. If he could get to them. But how?

He had a total of $3.40 in a jar on his desk. Like Mike, he didn't carry cash because until the "incident" five weeks ago when his mom had cut him off, he'd used a credit card whenever he wanted anything. Mike had talked about getting him a new one, but it hadn't happened yet because "you have to earn the privilege, Nicco." He had a suspicion his mom had shared how much Nick had run up on the bill during the month before he'd left.

Frowning, he glanced up and spied the paper held to the front of the refrigerator by a magnet that read, "Geology has its faults." The paper he'd studiously ignored until now. Picking up the phone again, he stood and snatched the paper, studying the list of unfamiliar numbers. His hands were steadier this time.

It rang twice. "Hola," a pleasant voice said.

"Rosa?"

"Sí. Quién es este?"

Not for the first time, Nick wished that his parents had taught him their native tongue. "What?"

"Nicholas?" Rosa said in her thick accent.

"Yes. Is—is Jo there? Josephina?" he clarified.

"Un momento." She covered the phone, but he could still hear her call for her daughter and rattle off a string of Spanish. The only thing he recognized was his name.

"If you're calling to apologize, forget it," Jo said as a greeting.

"Apologize?"

She grunted. "The fact that you obviously don't know what I'm talking about just proves what a jerk you really are."

"Listen, shut up with the sermon for a sec, okay?"

She didn't respond.

"Jo? Are you there?"

"You just told me to shut up, Jerk Wad."

He sighed. He really didn't need this at the moment. "I–I need your help. I'm in trouble."

He thought she wasn't going to answer again. Instead, when she said, "What's wrong?" her voice reeked of concern, which stunk way more than anger and sarcasm.

"It's kind of hard to explain over the phone. Can you come over here?"

"Now? It's ten o'clock at night!"

"So?"

"I can't leave now. Mama wouldn't allow it."

"Again...so? Just leave. Sneak out."

"I can't do that. Unlike some people, Nicholas, I respect my mother. I wouldn't deliberately disobey her."

Nick sank back down to the floor and pressed shaky fingers to his eyes. "My dad is...he's not here, Jo, and I need help. I don't know where else to turn, okay? My mom won't... you're the only...," he stopped. It was hard to admit to himself, let alone say it out loud, but he did. "You're the only person I know that can help."

"Really?" There was a long pause then the sound of rustling. When she spoke again, she was whispering. "Okay, maybe I disobey her once in a while. But, it'll take me a while to get out without her noticing, so why don't you come here?"

"I need to talk to my grandma. She may be able to help."

"Where is she?"

"Fountain Creek Assisted Living. I don't know the address."

"I can look it up while I'm waiting on you."

"I don't have cab fare," he blurted, shame coloring his cheeks.

"I thought you were rich."

Nick toyed with the strings on his sneakers. "Yeah, well, my money's all tied up in investments. I'm just not very liquid right now."

Jo laughed softly. "Okay, okay. I'll have to dip into my babysitting stash, but I can get us there."

"Where do you live?"

"It's not far." Jo gave him her address and directions.

Thirty minutes later, Nick was reflecting on the fact that apparently, he had lived a more or less privileged life. Not everyone could afford to live on Chicago's Lake Shore Drive, but his mom could. Even here in this backwoods town of Colorado Springs, his dad lived in an exclusive neighborhood with a front gate, four-car garages, and in-ground pools. Nick wore designer clothes and had all the coolest gadgets. Nick took cabs. Sometimes, he took the El. The only time he'd ever ridden a city bus, he'd been with a group of his buddies. There'd been seven of them on a bus filled mostly with a bunch of elderly people traveling along the Magnificent Mile, which was not exactly Rush Street, an area known for its bars and parties. That night, he and his friends had talked and laughed loud, punched and shoved each other, cursed, put on quite a show for the rich old folks.

Nick looked around. This bus trip was different. Way different. The only other occupants were a man who talked out loud to himself and reeked of alcohol from half a bus length away; an old woman who glared at Nick while making squeaky noises with her tongue on her ill-fitting false teeth; two tattooed biker-types with shaved heads and goatees; and the driver, who looked like a military reject ready to snap at any moment. Every time the driver reached for the door lever, Nick flinched, expecting him to pull out an automatic weapon and aim it at the unsuspecting riders.

Then there was Jo. Seated next to him, she sat with her backpack on her lap staring forward as if lost in thought. The only sign of life was the movement of her jaw as she chewed a wad of gum. Nick studied her profile. She really was cute. In fact, if things were different...

"Do I have a booger hanging off my nose or something?" She turned her head and looked at him. "Didn't your mother teach you it's not polite to stare?"

But obviously, things weren't different. "When you said you could get us there, I thought you meant a cab."

Jo smirked. "Welcome to the real world, Rockefeller."

Nick turned away, staring at the back of the driver's head. "I think I prefer Jerk Wad."

"Fine by me." She smacked her gum then said, "So, what's going on? And by the way, just for the record, the only reason I'm sitting on this bus right now is because you said your dad was in trouble. It has nothing to do with you."

Other than the quick phone conversation, they hadn't talked about it. Nick was afraid to tell her what had happened. Then she'd be calling him Nutzo or Crazy Boy. Or maybe she'd just call the cops.

"What? It's such a secret you can't even tell it to the only person you know who can help?" Jo lobbed at him.

"No, it's not that. It's just...." He turned to stare out the window, but instead he saw his own reflection. "It's hard to explain."

"Why don't you start with who hit you." When he glanced at her, Jo nodded her chin to indicate his bruised cheek. "I think it's safe to assume your dad didn't do that." She frowned. "He didn't, did he?"

"Of course not." He looked down, trying to find a way to tell her, but he came up empty. "Do you always take the bus?" he said, picking at a ragged tear in the plastic-covered seat.

Jo frowned, studying him, then shrugged. "Mostly."

They rode the rest of the way in a silence punctuated only by the drunken man, who was now barking like a dog, and the old woman, who had moved to the seat across the aisle from Nick and was softly singing "pretty boy, pretty boy" to the squeaky beat of an old tongue against stained dentures.

When Jo touched his arm and said, "The next stop," he could have wept with relief.

Fountain Creek Assisted Living was a long six blocks from the bus stop. Stepping off the dark sidewalk into the shelter of the royal blue awning and soft amber light spilling out from the glass doors, Nick felt a load lift from his shoulders. Smiling at the red plastic geraniums, he realized he had Jo to thank. If it hadn't been for her, he never would have made his way across the strange town. Debating whether he should thank her or just let it pass, he grabbed the front door and tugged.

"Crap," he muttered.

"What?"

In answer, he jiggled the locked front door.

"Uh-oh. Look at that." Jo pointed to a key pad mounted under a sign that told them the doors remained locked after 9:30 p.m.

Nick could feel her watching him as he cupped his hands around his face and pressed his nose to the glass. There was no movement inside, no smiling volunteer sitting at the reception desk, no residents congregating in their wheel-chairs to keep track of who had visitors.

Jo sighed, "Now what?"

Stepping away from the glass, Nick looked around and considered his options, which appeared to be limited. Maybe he could pound on the doors and persuade whoever answered that there was an emergency. Glancing at Jo, who was pushing buttons on the key pad, he realized that an adult would assume that two teenagers hanging out at night were up to no good. Instead of opening the door, they'd probably just call the cops. Just like the time the manager of that fast food restaurant found Nick and his buddies hanging out back of the building where the employees–

"I've got it."

"You know the code?" Jo said raising her eyebrows at him.

He shook his head. "Even better. Follow me."

Nick and his friends had found out the hard way that the only place employees at the restaurant could smoke was behind the building. No matter where you went, it seemed like someone smoked. The same had to be true at Fountain Creek Assisted Living, which meant that the employees had to smoke somewhere. Nick was guessing that the "somewhere" was behind the building, a hidden corner tucked out of sight of residents and visitors.

When he saw the dented Maxwell House coffee can half-full of sand and cigarette butts, he knew he was right. He felt a flame of pride. Jo might have gotten them here, but he had a few tricks up his sleeve, too.

Nick grinned at her and pointed to the door marked "Employees Only." Someone had folded up one of the facility's pamphlets and shoved it between the door latch and the jamb, preventing the door from locking.

"They don't even bother using a key," Jo whispered. "That has to be against the rules."

As he opened the door and eased inside, he smirked. Little Miss Perfect Jo, as if they weren't breaking the rules by sneaking inside a locked building.

"By the way," Jo murmured as she slipped in behind him, "where's your dad?"

The flame of pride flickered and went out as he heard the echo of the words, *"I don't know that man."* Nick glared at her. "He's...he's not here. He, uh, left town. It was a last minute thing." Even to his own ears, it sounded like a lie. "Now, come on."

Nick turned away and slipped down a dim corridor towards his grandma's wing. Hoping to escape the notice of any nurses, he also hoped to escape the unpleasant thought of what Mike might be going through at that very moment. And Simon. He hoped the kid hadn't gotten in too much trouble with that maniac Elliard. Then, with a mental shrug, he dismissed the thought. The kid deserved whatever he got. He was the one who chose to live with that bunch of psychos when there had to be better options.

They made it to Grandma Carlota's room just as a nurse in blue scrubs came around the corner. Hurrying, they slipped into the room and closed the door behind them. Even in the dimness of the moonlight peeking through the slats of the closed blinds the room was depressing. There were two beds with hunched forms on them. From across the room, came the stuttering wheeze of the crazy roommate's snoring.

He stepped close to Carlota's bed, peering down at the slack, wrinkled features, searching for something he couldn't describe. Hesitantly, he placed a hand on her blanketed shoulder. Jo hugged her backpack to her chest and stared at his grandmother's sleeping face as Nick gently shook the bony joint. "Grandma," he said softly.

Carlota grunted and smacked her lips.

He shook her again. "Grandma Carlota."

She came awake slowly, her eyes opening, blinking, then staring up at him through the darkness. She smiled. "Fidel? Fidel, is that you?"

Nick frowned. "No, Grandma. It's me. Nick."

"Nicco?" Concerned, she struggled to raise herself up on one elbow. "What is going on? Where is your father? My Miguel, has something happened to him?"

"No, Grandma. Everything's fine. It's just," Nick stopped. It was just what? What did he think his grandmother could tell him? He must have paused too long, because Jo nudged him with a sharp elbow as if to speed him along. He frowned at her then turned back to his grandma. "I need to know about the traveling. You know, to other worlds." From behind him, Jo gasped. "The thing we were talking about earlier."

Jo was tugging frantically on his sleeve, but he ignored her.

"You have brought a friend, Nicco? Who is she?"

Jo edged closer. "Hi. I'm—"

Nick cut her off, pretending not to notice her glare. "You said you saw Grandpa Fidel do it once. What did you see?"

At the mention of Fidel's name, Carlota stopped her study of Jo and looked at him. Really looked at him. "It was a strange thing. I saw my Fidel and then he was...," she paused as if searching her mind for the right word then flapped one hand in the air. "He was wavy. Then everything went in half. Into porcíon. Pieces." She smiled. "I know it sounds loco, Nicco. I know no one believes me. But you do, yes?"

He nodded. "Yes, Grandma. But I need to know wh—"

"Hey! What are you doing here?"

Nick jumped at the strange voice and at the hand that suddenly clamped down on his shoulder. Turning, he saw that the same person holding him was also holding Jo. He started to struggle then froze when he saw the face of his captor. "You!"

Miriam smiled past him and Jo. "Miss Carlota, you go back to sleep. This is all just a dream."

"A dream?" Carlota muttered.

"Yes, dear." Miriam nodded, her frizzy, red hair quivering in the dim light. "You'll remember nothing of it come morning. That, I promise." Then the smile was gone and she glared at Nick. Saying nothing, she tugged him and Jo into the small, adjoining bathroom and shut the door. In absolute darkness, she let go of him. Before he could react to his freedom or think of an excuse for being here at night, he was overwhelmed by the harsh glare as she flipped on the light over the sink.

"What are you doing here?" she repeated.

He was once again captivated by the unpleasantly long face and lady bug barrettes. It struck him that everything about her seemed out of place, as if she had been hastily, haphazardly assembled. "I had to see her," he managed to say, unable to think of a reasonable lie.

"No." She shook her head and gave Jo a quick sideways glance. "What are you doing *here*?"

Nick frowned. "Are you deaf or something? Like I said, I had to...," then he stumbled to a stop. "Oh, you mean, what am I doing here, as in, on Earth."

Miriam grimaced and gave Jo a quick, insincere smile. "I hate that word. It makes this place sound so inconsequential and so one dimensional."

"Uh, yeah." Jo looked uncomfortable. "Sure. Okay. Nick, I'm thinking maybe we're done here. Maybe it's time we took off."

"I need to know what's going on," Nick said, ignoring Jo. "How we got there. How I find Mike. How we get back home… together."

Miriam turned her head in slow motion, her eyes settling over him like a winter fog moving ashore from Lake Michigan. He shuddered beneath the chill gaze, feeling it in the pit of his stomach. "You need to know what I tell you, Nicholas. Nothing more. And for now, this is all I may offer: You will learn like the ones before you. On your own. Hard lessons. Things such as how it feels to betray someone, to leave someone behind."

Nick gulped and glanced at Jo who was standing with her mouth hanging open and her backpack held in front of her like a shield. "I didn't know what else to do," he mumbled. "I thought…" He frowned, and his brown eyes sought out and held the cold, green gaze. "Wait a minute. How do you know what happened?"

Miriam smirked and a stubby finger tapped the corner of one eye. "I am not a Watcher for nothing, am I?"

"A Watcher?"

"Okay, then," Jo mumbled, sliding unobtrusively towards the door. She stopped short and shot a desperate look at Nick when Miriam shifted her body to block her escape.

"How soon you forget, Nicholas," Miriam said. "I told you, there is a Watcher always. Remember?"

As soon as she said it, he did. He remembered her saying it during their first meeting. "If you were there, then why didn't you do something to help?"

Her expression was unreadable, and her tone was flat when she said, "Why didn't you?"

Nick had no answer, and any anger he felt towards her was washed away in a wave of guilt. "So, what was I supposed to do? Let them bash me in the head and drag me off, too?" When the green eyes didn't waver, he repeated softly, "What was I supposed to do?" He swallowed hard under her unforgiving stare. "What am I supposed to do? I don't understand."

"A Watcher watches. A Traveler...," Miriam's voice trailed off with a sad smile.

"Travels," Nick said mostly to himself. He studied her horse face again. She wasn't as ugly as he'd first thought. In fact, there was something compelling in her features — a riddle as mystifying as her words. Both begged an answer. "I have to go back, don't I?"

She didn't answer.

"But, what about Mike? What's going to happen to him?"

Miriam shrugged. "It's up to you."

"And Grandpa Fidel? What about him?"

"You hold the key." She opened the bathroom door and made as if to leave then hesitated. "Nicholas, one more thing. Beware the Dark Watchers."

"Dark Watchers?"

"We are not always what we appear or what we were meant to be." And with that, she slipped out the door.

As the latch clicked behind her, Nick pulled the coin from his pocket and clutched it in his hand. He had no choice. He hadn't learned much, not nearly as much as he'd hoped, but Miriam had confirmed one thing: He had to go back. He had to fix what he'd done, even though the thought of it made him feel sick to his stomach. He had to find Mike. Talk to Simon.

"Is this what all Chicagoans do for fun?" Jo's voice quivered slightly. "They sneak into old folks' homes and hide in toilets with crazy nurses? Because as interesting as it's been, getting the heck out of here and getting home before my mom finds out I'm gone works for me."

Lost in thought, Nick simply stared at her. As much as he didn't want to admit it, he really didn't want to do this alone. The coin warming his right hand, he laid his left on Jo's shoulder.

She jerked away, scowling. "Hands off, Sanchez."

"Are you up for a little adventure?" he said and grabbed her wrist.

"Let go of my arm or you're going to have a little misadventure." When his grip on her tightened, Jo's frown intensified into a look of disgust. "You're not going to try and kiss me, are you?"

The buzzing began, and despite the circumstances, Nick chuckled nervously. He squeezed the coin tighter, fighting off the urge to scratch his tingling skin. "Even better," he promised her as the welcoming pulse sounded and the warm air split around them.

CHAPTER 6

IN THE SHADOW OF THE
SHADE RUNNER

They were standing in an alleyway similar to the one he and Mike had landed in the first time around. Maybe it was even the same one. But this time, it was nearly dark and there was a mist in the air that was heavy with the smell of the sea. It was either dawn or dusk.

"Okay, that was…," Jo's mouth opened and closed noiselessly like a goldfish searching for its next meal. Arms wrapped protectively around her backpack, she stared wide-eyed at their dim surroundings and mumbled something in Spanish.

Struggling with his own emotions, Nick whispered, "What?"

She lowered her voice. "What the heck was that and where are we? Did you drug me or something? Is that part of your bad boy act? Because," she paused, suddenly sounding unsure, "I thought it was just an act." Her next words were spoken between clenched teeth. "I'm warning you, if you gave me something, you've crossed the line."

He slipped the coin into his pocket and took a step towards her. She glared, tightened her grip on her backpack, and shuffled backwards. He should probably do something — give her a reassuring pat on the back, maybe squeeze her arm — but he could no more translate her body language than he could her Spanish. He didn't know whether she was angry, afraid, getting ready to slug him, preparing to run, or all of the above. Besides, he was as unsettled as he had been the other two times he'd traveled between home and this place. So, he settled for a murmured, "Are you okay? No drugs. I promise."

Jo studied him a moment then blinked and slowly turned in place, taking in their surroundings and completing a full circle before staring at him again. "Nick?" Her voice gave him the translation he needed — she was scared. Well, that was reasonable. So was he.

He needed to say something; he should probably apologize or at the very least give her an explanation. Instead he spat, "You shouldn't have come."

"I didn't come. You dragged me here." She lifted her chin and straightened her shoulders, but he saw the shimmer of tears building in her dark eyes. "If you don't want me here — wherever here is — then why'd you bring me?" She swiped away the glaze of tears with her arm.

The glimpse of vulnerability surprised him. He'd never seen Jo act anything but tough and self-assured. It threw off the bantering they relied on to communicate. He studied the scuffed toes of his tennis shoes then surprised himself when he looked her in the eyes and said truthfully, "I'm not sure. I guess I just didn't want to come by myself."

"Oh." She slung her backpack over one shoulder, and sounding more like herself said, "Well, that answers that. Now, where are we and why are we whispering?"

He glanced around, trying to determine if they really had been dropped in the same location as he and Mike, but it was impossible to tell. Through a mist as sheer as a cobweb, he spied rotten boards on the nearest building, and further down, he could just make out a crumbling brick wall. For a panicked moment, he thought they were standing near

Simon's courtyard. Sweat beaded up to greet the mist settling on his forehead. Without thinking, he touched his bruised cheek with his fingertips then flinched when something brushed against his arm.

Jo had inched closer and was staring at him. "What's the matter with you?" she whispered. "You look like you just saw a ghost or something."

He had, but he snapped, "I'm fine." He could hear the uncertainty in his voice and knew she could, too. He covered it up with a cock-eyed grin. "Welcome to Tempest," he said with false cheer.

"Tempest? So, your dad is here somewhere." When he frowned at her, she shrugged. "I gathered from your weird bathroom conference with that creepy nurse that Dr. Sanchez is lost here." When he gave a nod of confirmation, she said, "And here would be where exactly?"

"Exactly?" He shook his head. "I don't know, but I'm guessing it has something to do with traveling across the Einstein-Rosen Bridge into another dimension. I didn't have much time to research it before you interrupted me."

Her forehead puckered, but she let his jab slide. "You guess? Another dimension? Are you serious or are you just being more of a jerk than usual?" When he didn't answer, she looked around again, stepping even closer as she did so. The hand holding the strap of her backpack tightened. "Another dimension? That's crazy."

"Yeah."

"And, just for the record, Sanchez," she gave him a smile drawn tight by anxiety, "it's also the coolest thing that's ever happened to me."

"Yeah. Me, too," he agreed. For the first time in hours, Nick relaxed just a little. His body ached from his earlier encounter with Elliard, and he took a deep breath to clear his head. The air smelled like the ocean and the mist was thick with the taste of brine, but he couldn't hear the waves lapping. They must have landed somewhere within the maze of alleyways that he and Simon had raced through when they'd fled from the men who'd taken Mike.

At the thought of Mike and the crimps, of what his dad might be going through, he tensed again. Nick drew himself up to his full height and looked carefully at the dilapidated backdrops. No one was in sight. For the moment they appeared to be safe, but he knew from experience that safety was an illusion that could evaporate more quickly than the mist.

Feeling Jo's eyes on him, Nick paced to the other side of the alley and back, avoiding looking at her. She was probably waiting for him to tell her what they should do. If so, she was right — they needed to do something, and do it soon.

"We have to find Simon," he finally announced.

"Okay. Simon who?"

"He's a kid I met here. He helped me, and he's the only one I know who may be able to take us to Mike."

"Any idea where we can find this Simon character?"

Nick shrugged and squinted up at the narrow strip of sky. It was growing lighter, so dawn, not dusk. "I don't know. Last time, he found me. Maybe if we head towards the main street, we'll spot him. And keep on the look-out for something called a Shade Runner, because that's where the crimps took Mike."

"Shade Runner? Crimps?"

Nick shook his head. "I have no idea what a Shade Runner is. As for crimps, that's what Simon called the men who took Mike. All I know for sure is this, avoid the crimps and if you meet a guy named Elliard who looks like he was raised by wolverines, don't stop and ask questions. Just run."

"Shade Runner, crimps, Elliard, and wolverines. Got it."

"Good. Then let's go."

It took a while and a whole lot of wrong turns and sheer luck, but Nick finally led them to the place where he'd last seen Mike. He scanned the dirt, but if there had ever been any tell-tale blood or scuff marks, they'd been obliterated. Peeking around a front corner of the store that Mike had gone into for directions, Nick spotted the paper nailed to the post. The notice about the gathering of shades, whatever that meant. The paper he'd been reading when Simon had appeared. They were in the right place.

"I hear waves." Jo whispered. She was standing behind him, pressed against the wall of the building, and looking over his shoulder.

"Yeah," he said, only then noticing the rhythmic sound of the ocean. He also heard the call of a gull and then another. The world was awakening.

Jo added, "It smells like a fish market."

"Uh-huh." He wondered what she'd say when she got a look at the residents of this wacko place. "Just be sure to keep out of sight and keep your voice down."

She scowled at his order and deliberately stepped away from the safety of the shadow of the store.

"Get back," Nick hissed. He grabbed her around her waist and yanked her backwards. "What's the matter with you? I told you to stay out of sight. It's not safe."

"Did you see that?" She looked at him, her eyes the size of quarters. It was a testimony to her shock when she didn't immediately demand he let go of her waist and punctuate the order with a sharp jab to his ribcage. "There's like a cowboy and a wagon and a horse and...and...stuff that shouldn't be there. Like in the movies."

He shrugged. "I told you, we're not in Colorado Springs anymore."

"Would she be yer sister then?"

Nick spun around at the familiar voice, dragging Jo with him. As if suddenly realizing she was being held, Jo brushed his hands off in one smooth motion and jabbed her elbow into his unprotected side. "Let go," she ordered.

"Ow!" Nick released her as if he'd been stung then looked at the boy standing in the shadowy alleyway. "How long have you been here?" he gasped.

"Not long. So, who be she?" Simon was sporting a black eye, and he held himself at an awkward angle, protecting his ribs with his scrawny arms. Despite all that, he gave Nick a huge smile of genuine delight.

"She be Jo, the closest thing he," Jo nodded towards Nick, "has for a friend. You must be Simon since you don't seem like the wolverine type."

Simon's face flushed. "Yes," he managed and gave Nick a sheepish glance. "But, she be a girl."

Nick chuckled, more at Jo's grunt of disgust than at Simon's odd statement. "Really? I hadn't noticed." His sentence was punctuated by another elbow in the ribs. If Jo kept jabbing him, she'd finish the job Elliard had started. He eyed the fresh bruising on Simon's face. "Did Elliard do that?"

Simon shrugged. "It does not matter."

Nick exchanged a worried glance with Jo. "Simon, we need your help. I have to find my dad. You told me he'd been sold and taken to a Shade Runner, but I don't know what that means. Can you take us to him?"

Simon's dark eyes met Nick's, and he hesitated long before answering. "Aye, I can be showing you." Slipping past Nick and Jo, Simon scurried in the building's shadow to the store front. He studied the street. "I be showing you, but there be danger. There always be danger." He glanced over his shoulder at them. "She should stay. If you be not gathered, we can be coming back for her."

"No!" Jo and Nick said at the same time.

Simon's eyes widened with surprise. He looked at Nick. "There be men who might," he swallowed, "they might not be so nice like me. Not to a girl."

Nick met Jo's steady gaze. The only sign of nervousness was the slight quiver in her voice when she said, "I don't want to be separated. I'm going with you."

Nick gave a slight nod before turning back to Simon. "The Shade Runner?"

Simon pointed across the street towards the open water that peered back at them from an alleyway that mirrored the one they stood in. "She be that way. At the end of the pier. Waiting in the harbor for her master's order."

"The Shade Runner is a boat?" Nick said.

Simon's only answer was a quiet order to "Come" as he sprinted across the dirt road that was, apparently, Tempest's main street.

With Jo close behind, Nick stuck like a wad of used gum to Simon's heels. He hesitated only when Simon stepped onto a dock with a confidence that felt as flimsy as the water-logged boards beneath their feet. Like a splintery beach, the dock met the ocean and ran in each direction as far as Nick could see, jutting out at irregular intervals into narrow piers where row boats and canoes bounced on the tide, straining against their tethers. In sharp contrast, several hundred feet away rested the sedate outline of a large sailing ship. The only sign of life on the ship was a cloud of sea birds swooping and swirling around the tall masts.

"Skullers," Simon muttered.

"What?" Nick looked over at the younger boy, who shuddered as he stared at the swarm of birds.

"The skullers always be liking the gathering. Better even than the fisher boats," Simon added as he walked in the direction of the sailing vessel.

His heart battering the inside of his ribcage, Nick pulled his gaze from the ship and followed close to Simon, turning a careful eye on the characters lounging around the pier. They were all male, at least he was guessing they were, and they all looked like they'd just rolled out of bed fully clothed. To a man, they obviously hadn't seen a bath or a razor in weeks and most had eyes swollen from what Nick suspected was a night of drinking. As red-rimmed stares drifted their way then followed their progress along the dock, Jo brushed against his arm, staying as close as possible.

Nick hated being the center of attention, and right now, he felt like he was quickly becoming the main attraction at a freak show. Curious eyes took on a hostile glare as they made their way down the boardwalk. He thought of Mrs. Crandall, who taught history. She'd said that in some cultures, making direct eye contact was considered a challenge. Nick dug his hands deep into his pockets, hunched his shoulders, and kept his eyes lowered.

Out of the corner of his eye, he spotted one old salt sharpening a wicked looking knife as the sun lifted over the waters. The filthy man grabbed a bright blue fish from the heap piled around his crusty boots and with a swift flick of the blade, a mound of slimy, multi-colored guts spilled across the dock. Nick swallowed the bile burning the back of his throat.

"You've never cleaned a fish, have you, City Boy?" Jo whispered, flashing him a foxy grin despite how obviously uncomfortable she was with their present situation.

"They tend not to like it when you do that at Shedd's Aquarium." Nick scowled, trying to ignore the glare the old fisherman aimed in their direction. "Can't you act like a guy, or something?" he hissed at Jo. "People are staring."

"Act like a guy? What's that mean, I'm supposed to walk and talk like a clumsy, self-centered jerk?"

Before Nick could respond, Simon interrupted in a strained voice, "There she be." Nick followed Simon's gaze and found himself staring up at the bow of a black ship anchored alongside one of the long piers. "A Shade Runner," Simon stated, his voice nearly drowned by the raucous cawing of the birds filling the sky over the boat.

Overwhelmed by the size of the ship, it took a moment for Nick to comprehend the boy's words. "Don't you mean *the* Shade Runner?"

"No, he don't." Nick jumped at the seemingly disembodied voice before spying a fisherman sitting on the pier in the shadow of the huge ship. Hairy calves dangling over the edge of the boards, the man grunted when a large splat of bird poop landed on his knee. Reaching inside the neck of his shirt with short, fat fingers, he pulled out a limp stocking cap. With a grumble of impatience, the fisherman forced the dirty cap over his frizzy red hair. "In fact," he continued, "this particular Shade Runner be the seventeenth. She run from Bridge End to Tempest. And back, of course."

For one brief moment, Nick's eyes met those of the fisherman. In the green depths, he saw a flicker of familiarity, a darkness deeper than the water lapping around the man's ankles. 'He knows things,' Nick thought. 'Bad things.' Wondering where the thought came from, he managed a soft, "Of course."

Forcing his eyes from the fisherman's disturbing gaze, Nick looked up at the ship once more and saw that the stranger was right at least about one thing. The words "Shade Runner XVII" were branded into the side of the massive wooden vessel.

"There be the Bosun." Simon nodded towards a dark figure standing on the ship's deck near the wide gangplank that connected the ship to the pier.

Nick stared up at the imposing figure. He didn't know what a bosun was, but the man's silhouette was hostile, from the wide stance and the fists resting on his hips to the wicked looking whip tucked into his belt. "Are you sure they brought Mike here?" he said hopefully to Simon. "Couldn't they have taken him somewhere else?"

"Aye, he be here. Where else would they bring him? After all," looking around, Simon lowered his voice until it was masked by the lapping of the waves and the call of the birds, "the Keeper awaits the Gathering."

It wasn't the first time he'd heard or seen that word. "The Gathering?" he said, and the old fisherman cleared his throat noisily. Nick looked at the man, but before he could say anything more, Jo spoke up.

"It's certainly not what I'd call a beauty," she criticized, her eyes roving over the ship and her fingers tugging at something inside the neck of her shirt. "It looks like it'd sink in a strong wind. But, if Simon is right about Dr. Sanchez being here, then we have to get aboard." Belying her casual words were her darting glances and the fact that she now had an iron fist wrapped around a crucifix that she'd pulled from inside her shirt. When she noticed Nick staring at her, Jo frowned and slipped the chain and the cross back inside her shirt. "What?"

Oddly, it made Nick feel better to know that Jo was as scared as he was. He shook his head, and feigning a confidence he didn't feel, he announced, "Then let's do it."

"Laddie," the fisherman said, and Nick looked at him. Red hair exploded from the bounds of his cap and the man looked like he was bursting to speak. When he finally mumbled only, "Mind ye take care," Nick was disappointed.

Turning his back on the fisherman, Nick strode to the foot of the gangplank, and with an assurance he didn't feel, yelled "Ahoy!" to the man Simon had called the Bosun.

The shadowy figure cocked his head in Nick's direction, but otherwise didn't respond.

"Ahoy?" Jo giggled nervously as she stepped up behind him. "Who are you? Captain Ahab?" she whispered.

Nick frowned at her. "You got a better idea?"

"How about you just ask?"

Nick grunted, but looked again at the man blocking the top of the gangplank. "Uh, mind if we come aboard?" When there was again no response, he plastered a large smile on his face. "Please."

Nothing.

He glanced at Jo. "Any other great ideas? Maybe he doesn't speak English."

Jo frowned, obviously thinking it over before saying, "Yeah, well, let's try a universal language then." She fished in her backpack then pulled out a king-sized Snickers bar.

"A bribe?" Nick smirked, but wondered why he hadn't thought of the idea himself.

"Who doesn't like chocolate?"

"What be chocolate?" Simon said.

Nick choked back a chuckle, but Jo simply shrugged and held up the candy bar toward the Bosun. "Excuse me, sir? I have something for you. It's good." When she took a step onto the gangplank, the man stiffened and a hand came to rest on the whip's handle. Jo stepped back beside Nick.

Nick sneered. "That went well."

Jo blew out an exasperated breath. "Look, chocolate's the best I've got. After all, I had to spring for the bus fare, remember?"

Simon shot anxious glances between them. "You must get onboard." They didn't react. "You have to!" he added then swallowed hard and shifted his gaze when both Nick and Jo looked at him with identical puzzled expressions.

"Whoa," Nick said. "Relax, big guy." Simon seemed more concerned about Mike than any of them, but why? Either he knew something bad was going to happen if they didn't get onboard, or there was something in it for him if they did. Wondering what Simon's motivation was, Nick reached in his pocket and pulled out its contents. He stared down at a single lint-covered Lifesaver that Elliard's gang had obviously overlooked when they'd robbed him earlier. He glanced at his companions with a rueful smile.

"What about your other pocket, Rockefeller?" Jo demanded.

Nick's eyes narrowed as he glanced over his shoulder. The red-haired fisherman was studiously avoiding looking their way, but Nick had the impression he was listening to every word. "You know," he murmured to Jo.

"I do?" She scowled at Simon. "So, why am I asking?"

Lowering his voice, Nick hissed, "Look, I've got the coin, okay?"

"The coin," Jo said flatly. "Is that supposed to mean something? What are you talking about?"

His teeth clenched, Nick pulled out the coin. "It brought us here." Frowning, he added, "At least, I think it did."

Simon's eyes were glued to the object on Nick's palm. "It will get you aboard," he said. When Nick didn't react, he added, "The Bosun be taking it. He will not be refusing." The street urchin snatched the coin and stepped past them onto the gangplank.

"Hey, give that back!" Nick ordered, but Simon ignored his companions and held out the coin toward the Bosun. Nick grabbed Simon's filthy shirt, yanking him back. "Give me that!" Struggling with his wiry companion, Nick pried the coin from Simon's grimy fingers. Once he had it back in his possession, he considered shoving the bothersome thief off the pier, but Jo's voice stopped him.

"Uh, Nick," she squeaked. When he looked at her, her huge eyes were locked on something behind and above him.

Turning slowly, he found himself faced with a wall of human flesh. Dirty, rank human flesh. Nick stumbled backwards, trying to put some distance between himself and the stench of the sailor. Tall for his age, Nick felt small and insignificant in the presence of the Bosun. His eyes stumbled over the man's pock-marked face, searching for a trace of compassion or kindness or maybe even curiosity. All he found was hostility oozing out of coal-black eyes set deep above a bulbous nose and coarse beard.

Nick glanced at Jo, but a barely visible grimace communicated clearly that she was as intimidated as he was. His mind running in place, Nick struggled to untie his tongue enough to yell "Run!" He had gotten as far as opening his mouth when Simon stepped forward.

Exhibiting an unnerving and altogether peculiar calmness given their present company, the boy informed the Bosun, "They seek passage aboard the Shade Runner."

Watching closely, Nick didn't miss the flash of surprise which threatened to destroy the man's poker face. But, in the blink of an eye, all traces of the emotion passed and the urge to run screamed louder.

"You wish to buy passage?" The Bosun's voice was as pitted as his face.

He wanted to say, 'No. No, I do not. I certainly do not want to buy passage.' Instead, Nick licked his lips and finally settled on a nervous nod.

"For one wench," the man's dark gaze raked across Jo before he added, "and one lubber?" The Bosun's eyes narrowed as he looked over his broad shoulder towards the middle of the ship. Nick followed his gaze, but saw nothing that would warrant the man's attention. Apparently, however, the man found what he was searching for within the shadows of the masts. He turned back to Nick. "The price be the key," he growled, his face brooking no arguments.

"Yeah, so I hear." Nick was tired of hearing about a key. According to Miriam and Elliard, he held it, and now this dude said it was the price. None of them made sense. "Look, I don't have any key," he admitted, wishing that he had the key to a way out of here.

The Bosun cocked his head, obviously confused. "Be ye having the price of passage?"

Nick shrugged. "I don't know."

"Ye be holding hard coin. I seen it with me own eyes."

Nick cleared his throat. "I can't give that to you."

"Can ye not?" Cruel eyes studied Nick's. "Waste my time, lad, and I'll take the price and the lass, and heave you to the fishes. After you be having a few lashes from me ole' friend, Whistler, of course." A heavy hand patted the butt of the whip leaving no doubt about Whistler's identity.

"Wait," Simon demanded. "If he proves true, I claim redemption."

The Bosun appeared darkly amused by the boy's boldness. "And if he proves not true?" The man chuckled. "I will remember ye, and ye will dance the hempen jig. That's me bonded promise, Urchin."

"Nick, did you...," Jo said softly.

"Not a word of it," he interrupted. He understood only one thing — their choices were severely limited. It was with a profound sense of dread that he watched the Bosun's gaze settle on him and a grubby hand reach out, palm up. Nick swallowed and handed over the coin. Sadness engulfed him like a fog when the coin disappeared in a meaty fist, but he had no choice. They had to get onboard. He would just have to figure out a way to get the coin back later.

The Bosun smirked as he gestured up the gangplank. "Get ye and the wench aboard then. We sail with the tide."

Nick and Jo walked slowly up the gangplank, stopping short of the place where it joined the ship. Nick could feel the huge presence of the Bosun following close behind them, blocking their escape. With a sinking feeling, he stared out over the deck of the ship. He saw only a handful of crew members, men who looked like shrunken shadows of the Bosun — underfed, filthy, and wearing clothes that were probably crawling with vermin. "It doesn't look like you have enough of a crew to sail a ship this big."

The Bosun's laughter was raw and ugly, out of place and unwelcome, as he shoved them forward. "Oh, we be having hands enough, I suspect."

When they stumbled onto the warped deck, Nick noticed that Simon hadn't followed. The realization was accompanied by a sense of dread and distrust so strong it propelled him to grab Jo's arm and turn back towards the gangplank — towards the pier, but he was blocked by the Bosun.

He stared up at the hate-filled face. "Simon's not coming?" Nick said.

The only answer was a shake of the head so slight he might have imagined it.

Stepping beside Jo who had moved to stand at the splintery rail, Nick stared down at Simon. The boy stood at the edge of the pier waving up at the ship. Despite doubting Simon's motives, Nick lifted his hand and tossed a half-hearted wave in his direction.

Jo frowned, her eyes searching the air between Simon and something behind them. "I don't think he's waving to us."

Nick quickly lowered his hand and studied Simon. Jo was right; Simon's intense gaze was focused on something else. Nick carefully followed the boy's line of sight towards the top of a tall deck in the middle of the ship where a lone sailor stood against a burnished mid-morning sun. Nick frowned at the gaunt silhouette of the man who appeared to be focused solely on Simon. Slowly, like a puppet on a string, a skeletal arm was raised in acknowledgment of the waving boy.

Nick shuddered and glanced at Jo, who gasped as she stared at the sight with wide eyes.

The man had no hand. His arm ended halfway between his elbow and where his wrist should have been.

His back turned to the pier, Nick didn't see the unforgiving hand that clamped down on Simon's thin shoulder. He didn't see Simon's pinched face or the eyes that fought back tears. He didn't hear the quiet, "He be aboard, Elliard. Did ye see?" And the even softer, "Years he be trapped, but now there be a chance."

Staring at the one-armed sailor, Nick failed to see Elliard turn narrowed eyes from the stained sails to the boy in his grasp. "Aye, perhaps." He was too far away to hear the dire warning, "But, we be having some unfinished business, young Simon, and ye will not live to see his release."

Nick turned just in time to see jagged fingernails dig into Simon's filthy, ill-fitting clothes as Elliard turned his back to the ship and dragged the struggling boy along behind him. He caught a familiar glimpse of a semi-circle of unforgiving feral faces cutting off any hope of escape for Simon.

Nick opened his mouth to call out, but he was silenced by the sight of the red-haired fisherman rising to his feet. Limp stocking hat askew, the man stared after Simon then turned his gaze up to Nick. Even from this distance, Nick could see the man's green eyes flash with righteous indignation. With a single shake of the fisherman's head, the circle of dread Nick felt for himself and Jo and Mike expanded to include the young street urchin, and he wondered if he'd ever see Simon again.

CHAPTER 7

HORNSWAGGLED

Nick's brain was struggling to comprehend everything that was happening around him — the reality of the ghostly ship beneath his feet; the menacing Bosun, whose stench testified to his hovering presence; the gaunt, one-armed silhouette standing somewhere above and behind them; his loss of the coin. And below them, Simon was in a desperate struggle for his life while Nick and Jo were forced to helplessly stand by. The same gang members who had closed in around Nick earlier were now closing in on Simon, who threw a frantic look towards the ship. As if he could somehow help, Nick stretched out his arm towards the boy then was yanked back as a large hand wrapped itself in the back of his shirt. The neck of his shirt pulled tight, threatening to choke off his air, Nick was lifted off his feet.

"Ye cannot be standing out here in broad sunlight, now can ye?"

"What are you doing?" Jo wheezed, and out of the corner of his eyes, Nick could see her feet swinging off the worn planks that formed the deck.

Gasping for air, he craned his head, but all he could see was a thick chest covered in several layers of filthy clothes. Swaying in the Bosun's grasp, he caught meager glimpses of parts of Jo — her feet, a hand, the strap of her backpack, a dark braid whipping in the breeze. Apparently, she was enduring the same ill treatment that he was.

With an ease that was frightening, the man carried them across the bow of the ship and tossed them onto the deck near a large chest. As they tried to catch their breath, the Bosun pulled something from inside his dingy shirt. It was a piece of twine that went around his neck; on it was strung a rusty key. He fumbled the key into a similarly rusty padlock securing a large chain around the chest. Rubbing his throat, Nick couldn't help but notice that the container was secured to the ship's rail with ropes that were as thick around as the Bosun's hairy arms.

"What are you doing?" Nick managed. He wondered if it was too late to run. His heartbeat pounded the answer against his chest, 'Too late, too late, too late.'

The Bosun smirked at him then turned an evil gaze at Jo. "Why, the Shades be having their pleasures with the likes of you two, would they not?"

"Shades?" Jo said, inching closer to Nick as she cradled her ever-present backpack.

"What are Shades?" Nick added.

"What be Shades?" The Bosun's stare was underlined by a soft growl. It took Nick a moment to realize that the growl was actually laughter. "Be ye daft?" the man said when the growl rumbled to a stop. A glitter in his dark eyes, the Bosun looked left and right before leaning close. "The Shades be hidden all around ye, lad, but they be coming for ye soon."

Nick coughed when he was hit with the man's breath, the only thing more rank than his body odor. "Oh, yeah?" Glancing at Jo, he drummed up false courage and forced a smirk on his face. "And what be they doing to us when they come?"

A scowl transformed the Bosun's face into a nightmarish mask. "Get ye in the box," he demanded opening the lid.

Jo's eyes widened. "Are you kidding?"

"No way, man," Nick said, scooting out of the man's reach.

Quick as the tongue of a hungry toad, the man's hand shot out and wrapped around Nick's arm. "In the box!" he ordered again and dragged a struggling Nick across the uneven boards towards the gaping mouth of the wooden chest.

Jo yelled in protest and jumped on the man's back when he yanked Nick roughly to him. Ignoring the teenaged she-devil clawing at his back, the Bosun forced Nick's face less than an inch from his own. The stinky breath and sea-ravaged features raised the hairs on the back of Nick's neck.

"Hear ye this," the Bosun hissed and miniature paint-balls of warm spittle exploded across Nick's face. "Mind me not and I be handing ye to the Shades me own self. They be slurping down ye souls before the flying jib be raised. Or, perhaps I be handing ye straight off to Captain Samael. Even the Shades be trembling in his wake." He shook Nick for emphasis. "On the Shade Runner, my word be law," he added. Nick grew quiet at the threat; Jo stopped struggling and lay draped across the man's shoulders like a braided shawl. The Bosun smiled. "Now, be ye crawling into the box or be we tossing yer empty skins to the tide?"

"Well," Nick cleared his throat, "since you put it so nicely..."

Darkness won over the light as the lid closed like a fish swallowing them whole.

Nick guessed they'd been in the box about an hour when he first noticed that Jo was all sharp edges. Elbows, knees, hands, feet, even her head — which at the moment was digging into his calf — seemed to have taken on bony points and ridges. Grunting, he shifted his weight and tried to turn onto his left side to give his right some relief.

Jo yelped. "Stop it!" she whispered.

"I can't help it," he whispered back. "My arm's numb."

"Well, try having a backpack wedged in your butt crack!" Jo grumbled.

Her sharp tone told Nick more about the state of her emotions than the foot that kicked him between the shoulder blades. He pressed on, ignoring her protests, until he was facing the other way. Had he not been entombed in a wooden chest, he would have been looking out across the ship's deck.

Scant shards of sunlight peering in through haphazard cracks in the boards provided just enough light to make out their shapes, not their features. With a sigh, Nick turned his head to stare at the black wall in front of him. Even with Jo's knees pressed into his lower back, he felt isolated.

If he had the coin, he could escape. Then again, if he did, Mike would probably be lost forever, and maybe Jo, too. Who knew if she would return with him when he left. After all, it had happened before — arrive with company and leave alone. The more he thought about it, the more selfish he felt. He should have thought about that before bringing Jo with him.

But even if Jo did go home with him, Mike would still be lost. Because if history repeated itself when Nick came back, he'd land somewhere in the town of Tempest and the ship with Mike onboard would have sailed to the Bridge's End, wherever that was. Anything could happen, since he was playing this game without a rulebook.

But, it was all irrelevant, because he didn't have the coin. He couldn't go home. None of them could.

If Simon had been telling the truth, Mike was somewhere onboard. Right now, it seemed like a pretty stupid thing to have trusted a kid he barely knew and walk blindly onto this ship with the hope of finding his dad. To make matters worse, now he and Jo were locked in a sweltering trunk on a rocking ship.

As the Bosun had slammed the trunk shut, he'd warned them to stay quiet if they didn't want the Captain or the

Shades to discover their hiding place. He'd promised to return for them. Nick could only hope that he would, but he had serious doubts. In the meantime, the muffled sounds of voices and movement on the deck were growing louder.

When Jo murmured, "How come you call him Mike?" he was startled to find that he'd been dozing and that the bars of sunlight peeking through the slats of their prison had inched lower.

To give himself a moment to gather his wits, he asked, "What?"

"I said, how come you call your dad Mike."

He tried to shrug, but he was too stiff and confined. Instead, he licked his dry lips. "I don't know," he said, which was a lie. But here, under these circumstances, his real reason — that it was his way of reminding Mike that he'd never been around and had never acted like a father — seemed trivial. "What do you call yours?"

Jo was quiet for a long time. He could feel the rhythmic rise and fall of her ribcage as she breathed. Finally, she said, "Nothing. I don't call him nothing."

Resisting the urge to correct her English, Nick frowned into the darkness and strained to see his companion's features. All he saw was a streak of light falling across a long, dark braid. "What do you mean?"

"Simple. I mean, I don't remember him. He left when I was just a baby."

"Where'd he go?"

"I don't know. Home, I guess."

"Where's home?"

"Mexico City." Her whisper was accompanied by a soft rustling followed by the sound of a zipper. "You want a granola bar?"

"You have food?"

"Uh-huh. And water."

"And water?" Here he was dying of thirst and she was hoarding food and drink! "Why didn't you say something?"

"I thought you knew. Besides, I figured we'd better make them last."

Even as he gulped down the dry granola bar and luke-warm liquid, Nick knew she was right. He also knew that while good grades had always been easy for him and despite her recent butchering of the English language, Jo seemed pretty smart, too. Reluctant as he was to admit it, she might even be smarter than him when it came to street survival.

After all, without her, he'd still be making his way to Grandma Carlota.

Jo twisted around and Nick took the opportunity to shift his own stiff body. "So, tell me," she whispered, "what did your grandmother and that crazy nurse mean about Travelers and Watchers? And who's Fidel?"

"Fidel was my grandfather," he told her. "As for the rest, I'm still not sure." But, he told her what little he knew — about the Einstein-Rosen Bridge, about Grandma Carlota's strange stories about his grandpa, and about his and Mike's first trip here. By the time he finished, the sun had slid halfway down the side of the wooden crate.

Silence stretched and took a deep breath before Jo said, "That's the craziest stuff I've ever heard."

"Yeah, I guess."

"I mean, who would believe that?"

Nick bristled. Considering they were locked in a trunk on the deck of an old sailing ship, you'd be crazy to not believe it. Right?

Jo continued undaunted. "Another dimension? It's just..." He couldn't see her clearly, but he knew she was searching for a word. "It's crazy."

"What's that supposed to mean?" he snapped.

"What's what supposed to mean?"

"What's crazy is that I'm stuck in here with you!"

"Keep your voice down," Jo hissed, kneeing him in the back at the same time. "What's your problem?"

His problem was that she had no right to call anyone crazy. He tried to scoot closer to the wall of the crate, wanting to put as much distance as possible between them. In the process, his hand brushed a wrapper of some kind. He picked it up, expecting it to be from the granola bar. When he maneuvered it into the slim bar of light, his irritation surged. A Snickers! Wadding up the paper, he threw it awkwardly at her. "Guess you don't take after your mom."

"And what's that supposed to mean?" she said, tossing his own words back at him.

"It means you need to learn to clean house."

"Why you—"

Whatever Jo was going to say was silenced by a nearby shout of "All hands on deck!" and a flurry of footsteps. He stiffened and Jo grabbed his ankle, hanging on tight. It sounded like a small army of men running around on the deck just outside their hiding place. When something heavy banged against the chest, they both gasped.

There were calls to raise anchor and release the lashings. A deep voice cursed and ordered someone named Pierson to attend to the jib sheets. Nick felt a rumbling emanate from somewhere deep within the bowels of the ship, accompanied by the baritone clank of a heavy chain. The rumbling and the clanking stopped simultaneously, followed by a loud bang then a yell of "Anchor home!" Pierson was again cursed and ordered to "Go abaft and see to the mizzen!"

Someone — presumably Pierson — replied with a meek "Aye, sir,"

There was a shuffle of feet and the bar of weak sunlight piercing the trunk blinked out. Without thought, Nick reached out and rested his hand on Jo's shin, reassuring himself he wasn't alone.

"Pierson best mind hisself. The Captain be watching." The man's voice was so close that he might have been kneeling by the chest and pressing his mouth to the wood. "On me life, sometimes, I swear he be not human."

Just when Nick was wondering whether the man was referring to Pierson or the Captain, an even closer voice replied, "Captain Samael be watching us all. Ye included." The tiny bar of sunlight flickered to life revealing that Nick was in fact touching Jo's thigh. He jerked back his hand just as the light once again disappeared. "We must be on guard lest we all find ourselves Shades at Bridge End."

"Aye," the other man murmured then his voice lowered further. "The ghastly creatures still be giving me the death shivers." Confirming the truth in the words, Nick heard a quaver in the soft voice.

"Then we'd best not give the Captain reason to take offense," was the calm reply before the voices disappeared amidst a flurry of shouted orders and curses.

Nick was no sailor, but even locked in the belly of the crate, he knew when the raised sails caught the wind. He sensed the Shade Runner lift herself in the water. He felt the blessed relief of an ocean breeze sifting through the cracks in the walls of the trunk as the ship sped along the surface of the water. Finally, the last narrow slat of sunlight winked out. Not long after that, there were no more scurrying sounds from the deck and the voices of the crew grew faint and relaxed.

They were asea. Sailing with the tide.

"Where do you think we're going?" Jo finally whispered.

"To where the Bridge ends."

She didn't question his answer, and eventually, they dozed.

Nick barely had time to process the sounds of a key being turned in a padlock, of a rope as thick around as a man's arm being dropped onto a wooden deck. When the lid of the trunk was thrown open, he was temporarily blinded by a full moon bigger than any he'd ever seen.

He had only enough time to register two things before their rescuer demanded his attention. First, Jo, too, appeared blind as she squinted up at the night sky. And, more importantly, her mouth was smeared with chocolate.

"By the Scribe!" someone growled down at them as the moon slid behind a curtain of clouds.

Nick blinked up at the silhouette of a man leaning over the open chest with one arm holding the lid open. Nick sat upright, as did Jo.

"Stowaways? On a Shade Runner?" the man mumbled, sounding shocked.

Nick wasn't sure what to do, so he waggled a hand and forced a smile. "Hello."

The man looked over his shoulder then back at them. "Since I be trapped in this nightmare, there has never been the likes of you. Why be ye here?" Something was wrong with his voice. Like his voice box was damaged.

"Uh..." then Nick's imagination ran dry.

"The Bosun," Jo said. "He did it."

The man grunted and took a step back. Nick and Jo took the opportunity to stand up. Nick's joints were stiff and his feet tingled as his blood began to re-circulate through his limbs. Jo slung her backpack over one shoulder. As they stepped out of the trunk, the man — made faceless by the dark — backed away, casting looks around him.

Like a shy child, the moon peered out from the protection of the clouds. Nick and Jo gasped simultaneously. The man's left arm ended halfway between the wrist and the elbow. It was the man who'd waved at Simon.

Nick felt hope glimmer like the pale moonlight on the rippled surface of the water. "Simon. You know Simon," he whispered.

The man's head tilted, listening.

"He's my frien...," he hesitated. "Well, I know him. He helped us."

In the dark, Nick saw the man's head tilt the other direction as if he were trying to make sense of what Nick was saying. Then, without warning, his head fell back, his jaw dropped open, and the one-armed man screeched.

Nick stumbled back, losing his balance as he slammed against the chest. Only the solid wood and Jo's nails digging into his arm kept him from falling. The sound coming from the man was inhuman, deafening and garbled. It reminded Nick of the howler monkeys at the zoo. The noise made his scalp crawl and the hairs on the back of his neck stand up. It took a few seconds to realize that the man was actually screaming words. Well, one word — over and over.

"Skins! Skins!"

Nick looked at Jo, who stared back at him wide-eyed. Without speaking, they reached an agreement.

They ran to the right.

The man reached for them, but he had no hand on that side with which to grab them. His stump merely banged against Jo's backpack. Jo and Nick stumbled across an uneven deck made more treacherous by the spray of the sea and the heaving of the vessel. Jo was in the lead. Her backpack swinging wildly with each step, she ran to the far side of the deck and grabbed onto the wet timbers of the rail running the length of the ship. Nick was on her heels.

He threw a panicked look over his shoulder just as the moon, which apparently had no desire to see the race's outcome, slipped behind a dense layer of clouds.

The sailor, who was still shrieking that horrible racket, had turned and was making his way towards them with an awkward, shuffling gait. He wouldn't be hard to outrun, but his cries would bring others out from wherever they were hiding. Even as the thought crossed Nick's mind, a light flickered in a window two floors up on the cabin in the center of the deck. That must be where the officers steered the ship or perhaps it was where the dreaded Captain Samael spied on the crew.

They ran past the huge center mast then slipped behind the cabin just as a door at the base of it opened. They didn't stop. Out of the corner of his eye, Nick saw a flight of steep stairs leading down to the pitch-black bowels of the ship and another leading to the upper reaches of the cabin. Jo kept running towards the back of the ship and Nick followed without protest.

"We've gotta get out of sight," he yelled, but the ocean breeze and the shrieking of the one-armed man shredded his words into unrecognizable tatters.

When they reached the last mast, Jo didn't hesitate. She leaped forward and shimmied up it as if she'd been sailing all her life. While she climbed, Nick took a deep breath and looked around. Towards the front of the ship, where they'd been locked in the chest, a half-dozen shadows moved. All but one moved like the sailor who'd discovered them, like the drunks who lurched along Chicago's Rush Street.

"Hurry!" Jo hissed.

Nick looked up to find she was a good ten feet above him. With a last look around, he scurried up after her. It was harder than she made it look. A growing wind tugging on his hair, he kept his ears attuned to the sounds below him. Thankfully, the inhuman bellowing had stopped, but he could hear men shouting and talking to one another from the far end of the ship. He kept his eyes focused upward, on the soles of Jo's shoes. His and Jo's grunts and gasps were loud in his own ears. He could only hope that the wind slung the sound of their climbing somewhere out over the ocean and not down to the crew below.

He glanced down at the deck and his heart momentarily seized — they were at least two stories up. When he looked back up, Jo had disappeared and he was staring at a large crossbeam and the tattered edge of a sail whipping in the wind. He frowned.

"Jo?"

"Up here," she said, peering out at him from beneath the sail.

He crawled up onto the crossbeam with her. It was just wide enough to sit on. They pulled up their legs, hugged the mast, and stared at each other. The sail and the absent moon would, hopefully, hide them from any searchers on-deck.

Her braids fluttering in the wind, Jo whispered, "Nick?" She sounded young and frightened.

"We'll be all right," he assured her, even though he didn't really believe it himself. He shifted his grip on the mast, wrapping his left arm over her right. Tossing spare glances to the deck far below, he strained to hear the sounds of the search party and silently prayed that they would get out of this mess alive and unharmed. "Yeah. We'll be fine," he mumbled.

Jo gave him a smile. Outlined in chocolate, it was obviously forced and tight, but — for once — she said nothing.

When they heard voices directly beneath them, they tightened their grip and held onto one another's gaze — not daring to look down and perhaps meet the eyes of one of the crew. The wind disguised the speakers' words until, eventually, they died out altogether and the only sound was that of the wind.

Holding onto the mast and each other, they rode out the sea and the night huddled in the wild flapping of the sail. It was hard to judge the passage of time, and so Nick didn't know exactly when the search below ebbed then faded away entirely. Like a curious bystander who wants to know what's going on, but doesn't want to get involved, the moon occasionally slipped out from the clouds before sliding back into hiding. And occasionally, despite trying not to, Nick and Jo nodded off, only to jerk awake. Unlike some terrible dream, the fear of falling was all too real.

Towards dawn, the wind picked up and the swaying of the ship increased. The vessel heaved from side to side and lurched forward and back. The endless rolling and bucking awakened the remains of the granola bar that had been resting in Nick's stomach. Fighting nausea, he tried not to think about how thirsty he was. Jo probably had another bottle of water, but there was no way he was going to let go of his hold on the mast to get it. His arms cramped from hanging on, his legs ached, and his butt burned from the constant friction with the wooden perch.

"Look," Jo said.

He followed her gaze. An orange sun struggled to rise beneath a large bank of black storm clouds. Distant lightning flashed, pale against the narrow band of sunlight. Nick looked up. The towering mast to which they clung reached for the clouds. It would act like a lightning rod in a storm. Another thing to worry about.

It was at that moment that the gulls, or skullers as Simon called them, arrived. They came by the hundreds from somewhere over the horizon to the left in a white stream as thick as smoke from a stack. In absolute silence, they lined up in mannerly rows on the ropes connecting the sails to the masts. Several landed on the rope stretched high over Nick's head. Then, like jurors, they stared, occasionally shifting position, ruffling feathers, and twittering softly.

When Nick looked at Jo to see if she'd seen them, she was frowning down at the deck.

"What?" he said as he followed her gaze. The deck was slowly being revealed by the dawn. Small, dark figures milled about; one walked towards the back of the ship, headed directly for their mast. The figure paused and raised an arm as a shield against the glare of rising sun, staring out at the distant storm.

Nick frowned and began to study the figures more closely. His mouth fell open and when he looked at Jo, she was staring back at him.

"Well, Rockefeller," she calmly announced, "I don't know about you, but I think we're in big trouble."

Nick wondered how she could act so calm about what the moon had hidden and the sun had revealed. He glanced back down to confirm what he thought he'd seen. He touched each sailor with his gaze in a silent accounting. No mistake. Had the sailor who'd released them from the chest been the same one who'd waved to Simon? He was no longer certain.

"Big trouble," he murmured.

The crew had more than a Captain and lurching in common. Every single one of them was missing a hand.

CHAPTER 8

TO FLEE OR NOT TO FLEE

They perched on the mast like the gulls, seeking refuge in a storm, trembling and vulnerable. Nick's limbs ached, his stomach growled, and he didn't know about his companion, but he really needed to pee. During the hours since dawn, the activity on the deck below had remained steady, affording them no opportunity to slip down from their roost. In the meantime, the sky overhead was darkening, and the roiling clouds tumbled ever closer. Lightning flared and thunder resonated its low-pitched warning. Salty winds whipped at the sails, making the dingy, ragged canvas thrash and snap like a mad terrier.

His mind churning along with the sea, Nick studied the figures below and tried to figure out the Shade Runner's secrets. The majority of the men — if that's what you could call them — were of the one-armed variety, but a small percentage, perhaps half a dozen men that he could see, appeared normal. Did they need his dad to help round out the two-handed crew? Was it some sort of slave ship like Nick had learned about in history class? Were they going to make Mike part of the crew once they were too far from shore for him to escape? Or, were they holding him hostage for some reason?

"Look," Jo hissed, jabbing him with a pointed elbow. She pointed with a shaking hand towards the dark stairwell that led like an artery into the belly of the ship.

Clinging to the mast, praying he wouldn't be torn from his hideaway, Nick peered through a jagged rip in the battered sail. He saw men — normal men with both arms intact — shuffling up the stairwell and onto the deck. They were hooked together like a row of shopping carts, bound by chains that declared them prisoners as much as the one-armed guards that prodded them forward.

Nick frowned, knowing he was seeing the bounty of the Shade Runner. So if his dad really was aboard, he wasn't the only one being held. But again, for what purpose?

"There he is," Jo said as the last of the chain emerged.

Nick let out a soft moan colored with relief, but glossed with despair. Mike trailed the end of the line like the limp tail of a homeless dog. Nick's mouth went even drier, too dry to swallow. Despite the uncertain light of the approaching gale, he could see terror etched in his dad's face, in the faces of all the prisoners. Tentacles of fear twisted and squirmed up the mast like a monster from the deep, touching Nick and Jo with its cold flesh, causing them both to shudder.

Her eyes glued to the scene below, Jo's voice was strained. "Do you...do you think those guys are the Shades?" They hadn't discussed the maimed crewmembers, but she didn't even have to clarify who she meant by 'those guys.'

Nick nodded once then shook his head. "Maybe. I don't know."

His stomach knotted as the Bosun's gravelly bark was carried up on the wind from the bow of the ship. "Get 'em back below, ye simpletons! The storm be licking our heels. It'll be on us by noontide, and by the Scribe, we be not having time to dally with winnowing."

It took Nick a moment to realize that the shrieking that followed the order came not from the raging wind and sea, but from the throats of the one-armed guards. It was the same sound they'd heard the night before when he and Jo had been released from their prison, only multiplied. If death had a noise, this was it. It was the sound of corpses calling out from the tomb. Nick winced and pressed one ear against the damp mast, wanting to deaden the sound. It didn't work.

Trying to stay calm, he peered at the guards through the flapping sail. He had never in his life seen men — if that's what they really were — so emaciated. They looked like mutilated skeletons, disguised as men in bad clothing, lumbering about on the deck. But it was more than their gauntness, missing limbs, drunken gait, and unearthly cries that left a foul taste of bile in his mouth.

"It's like they're not alive," he thought aloud. "Like something's been sucked out of them." Frustration etched his brow as he searched for a better description. "They look like road kill, or zombies, or something. Like," he squinted over at Jo, "like shadows."

"Shades," she murmured woodenly, still staring at the scene below. Nick could tell from her tone that she, too, was rattled by what she saw and heard. Before he could agree with her, Jo touched his wrist with cold fingers. "They're taking them back."

She was right. The lurching guards were leading their charges back towards the stairwell. Nick scanned the line of the prisoners. All but his dad were dressed in the same cumbersome, western garb he'd seen in Tempest, so obviously, Mike hadn't been taken simply because he looked like an outsider.

But, Mike did look different. He stood out like a Clydesdale at a Shetland pony convention. On the other hand, with his torn and dirty chinos and polo shirt, he didn't look like himself either — the man who was always impeccably groomed. He could have passed as a homeless beggar, certainly not the college professor that he was. Or had been, Nick's fickle emotions added.

It was hard to believe that the man at the end of the line was really his dad, and it wasn't the state of Mike's clothes or his missing glasses that caused him to question his father's identity. It wasn't even the scrapes and bruises marking his exposed skin, or the blood staining his shirt. It was the unfamiliar air of hopelessness that was apparent in the slump of his shoulders and the shuffling of his feet. Maybe, Nick hoped, it was simply exhaustion and the fact that he was roped in heavy chains. It might even be worry because Mike didn't know what had become of his son.

Nick shook his head...no, that probably wasn't it. In the face of his own problems, his dad had probably forgotten that Nick was living with him now. That he wasn't tucked away safely in Chicago.

Eyes locked on Mike's face, Nick silently ordered his dad to look up and make eye contact. To see...to see what? That Nick was okay? That Nick was there? He didn't know, but it didn't matter anyway, because Mike never so much as lifted his chin, let alone his eyes. Unaware of the stowaways, the line of men inched towards the black hole waiting to swallow them from view.

Thunder rumbled, punctuating the screeching fury of the sailors' cries and the Bosun's orders carried up to them on the erratic winds. The deck pitched wildly and the mast followed suit. Nick dug his fingers into the damp beam and watched helplessly as the stout prisoner directly in front of Mike stumbled and fell to his knees. The chains immediately tightened around the other men. Like a ripple in a pond, the man's fall slowly impacted the entire row of prisoners, causing them all to stagger and some to drop to their knees. Mike struggled to maintain his footing, but after several seconds, he hit the deck hard. The ship swayed and Mike slid as far as his irons allowed, away from the tangle of flailing flesh.

Pain carved deep furrows into his dad's features. Nick held his breath as Mike fought against the shackles, until he managed with great effort to get to his knees. A glimmer of the man Nick knew appeared when Mike's mouth moved and he extended a steady hand to the panicked prisoner in front of him who still floundered on the deck, continuing to bring others down with him. Powerless to help, Nick's fingernails sank deeper into the mast as Mike's hard won battle to regain his footing was lost when a thrashing leg struck out, knocking him awkwardly onto his side.

Before Mike could get to his feet, the Bosun was on them. Clutched in his meaty fist was Whistler, which uncoiled and snapped at the struggling prisoners. Nick shuddered at the gruesome sneer that burst open like a bloody gash in the Bosun's coarse beard. Cold eyes locked on the defenseless men, like a rattlesnake ready to strike a snared rabbit. Nick knew what was coming, even before Jo spoke, even before the first blow fell.

"Close your eyes," she ordered. "Close 'em right now, Nick."

His breath escaping in ragged gasps, Nick looked at her, his emotions bucking as wildly as the sea on which they sailed. Jo's eyes glazed with tears. He thought she was going to grab his hand, maybe stare into his eyes so they could focus on each other. But she didn't. Instead, she pressed her forehead into the mast and squeezed her eyes closed.

"Don't watch," she whispered, and he wondered who she was talking to — him or herself.

The crack of a whip and the tortured scream that followed nearly unseated him. He couldn't help it. He couldn't hear and not look. He tore his eyes from his study of Jo and watched as the whip rained down not on Mike, but on the man in front of him who'd caused the whole thing. Guilt stung him like seawater when he realized the corners of his mouth had turned up in a relieved smile, when he watched Mike curl his long body into a ball trying to avoid the lash himself.

Lightning flashed over the scene like a stage light and thunder cracked open the sky, releasing a deluge of rain. Like the windswept torrents, the Bosun's lash rose and fell, again and again. Maimed sailors and guards gathered close, watching in silent fascination. By the time the Bosun stopped, the victim lay limp and unmoving on the deck, and Mike's once pristine polo shirt was soaked with the other man's blood.

Slowly, the guards lurched forward. It took four of them, moving in a kind of graceless unison, to lift the body of the unconscious man. Others shoved the remaining chain of prisoners forward, and Mike, at the end of the line, was dragged awkwardly along. With grunts and gasps that could be heard even above the sound of the storm, the line staggered toward the steps into the hold.

"That man best be alive, Mr. Amherst," a deep voice declared. "Else, it will be your share from which his price will come."

With cold fingers, Nick eased open the tear in the sail, searching for the source of the calm voice which, with a few words, had halted all movement on the deck. Instead, his eyes settled on the Bosun who had stopped recoiling the now bloody Whistler and was staring toward the upper deck in the center of the ship.

"Better yet, if he dies, you will take his place before the Keeper," the voice continued, and the color drained from the Bosun's ruddy complexion.

"Aye, Captain! Aye!" Mr. Amherst eagerly shouted and replaced his sneer with a tentative, humorless grin. "He be alive. Just...just marked a bit."

Nick followed the Bosun's fearful gaze, his eyes furiously searching the shadows of the upper deck.

"I'll count on you to make sure he stays that way."

There! Nick saw him. The speaker. And if her indrawn breath was any indication, Jo had spied him, too. The man stepped out of a darkened doorway and casually rested gloved hands on the rail as if the downpour existed only in everyone else's imagination. He was tall and broad-shoul-dered. Close-fitting, dark clothes outlined a lean, hard body with all limbs intact. He wore a hat boasting gold braid and a deep brim that concealed his eyes. Unlike the Bosun, he was clean-shaven and his jaw looked like it had been chiseled from a slab of pale granite.

Captain Samael released his grip on the rail and turned to leave, but stopped when a low murmur ran through the group of ghastly sailors. Only a slight tilt of the dark hat told Nick that the Captain was staring down at the Bosun through the rain.

"Uh," Mr. Amherst's wet fingers toyed with the whip. "Captain, sir, the men be concerned about the storm."

"Men?" Nick heard the sneer in the Captain's voice and saw a hint of narrow lips curling up at the corners. "Need I remind you, there are no men under your orders. Only Shades. And I care less than nothing of their concerns." A gloved hand adjusted the hat, and the Captain's black eyes were suddenly revealed. A gaze colder than the wind whip-ping off the ocean pinned the Bosun to the deck and caused Nick to tremble.

The Captain chuckled, a harsh, wicked sound. "Do you expect me to soothe the seas, Mr. Amherst? If so, then you are a bigger fool than I thought. Only He who makes the storm can calm it, and only He can still the waves. Not I." The Captain turned to leave, but gave a final glance back at the Bosun and the Shades staring up at him through the driving rain and lashing wind. "Your hope is in vain," he said then disappeared through the door of the upper cabin.

The Bosun's thick chest heaved as if he'd been holding his breath, and perhaps he had been. Nick couldn't have blamed him. He felt the same way. He took a deep breath of his own as Mr. Amherst looked around and suddenly seemed to notice that everyone had frozen in place, even the prisoners. "Why be ye gawking? Take 'em below!" he ordered.

The few crew members who had both arms and walked normally suddenly got very busy, and the lurching Shades shuffled into slow action. Some tended to the ropes and sails, and some stayed mid-ship, while others wandered toward the front of the boat. Those guarding the prisoners shuffled down the dark stairs. Nick watched in silence as the limp body was dragged into the darkness and Mike was pulled head-first behind him, bumping his way into the belly of the Shade Runner.

"Hey," Jo's soft voice was full of compassion. When he didn't answer, she added, "At least we know your dad's okay. That he's onboard."

Irritated at her attempt to comfort, and furious at his inability to do anything, Nick hissed through clenched teeth as he struck the broad mast with a fist. "Just shut up!"

"Don't tell me to shut up," Jo hissed back. "I'm not the one who got us into this mess, General Custer."

"Custer? What's that supposed to mean?"

Jo's answer was to lift her chin and meet his gaze with flashing brown eyes.

"You think I'm a coward? Is that what you're saying?"

Hesitantly, she gave a slight shrug. "It means whatever you want it to," she mumbled and turned away, quite literally giving him a cold shoulder.

For a long time, he stared at the back of her head, willing her to call back her words, or at least explain them. Was she calling him a coward? What did she expect him to do? Stand up on the mast and demand that they release his father! And, oh yeah, hand over my magic coin while you're at it! Nick snorted softly.

Then it hit him. Maybe she was saying this was all his fault. He'd led them into an ambush as surely as General

Armstrong Custer had led his men to their death. He frowned. If that was what she meant then Jo was right.

Nick slumped and closed his eyes. Weak and shaken, he leaned into the strength of the mast. Jo was silent, but he could feel her presence. They were sitting only a few inches apart, but a gulf existed between them. What did they have in common? Why had he even wanted her here? They were from two different worlds. In fact, he didn't even really like her.

So, he ignored her, and simply listened to the sounds of the Shade Runner slicing through the storm and the waves. He wasn't sure how long they sat like that — back to back, but it was long enough for a deep muscle cramp to latch onto his right thigh. He took a deep breath, let it out slowly, and shifted his weight on the crossbeam.

He'd come up with a plan, and part of that plan included pretending he didn't hate Jo. That he couldn't wait to be off this old boat and be rid of her. He glanced at her and was surprised to find her staring back at him. The wind had tangled her braids into a glorious knot beneath her face. Her eyes were huge and her skin unnaturally pale. He suddenly realized she was pretty. Maybe even beautiful. Nick scrubbed his face with a shaking hand then flinched when lightning streaked by overhead.

"We've gotta get down," he said. "We can't stay up here in the middle of a storm."

Jo's taut features relaxed a tad. "True. Between the storm and the crew..."

"...and our luxury accommodations," Nick managed.

"Most definitely a room with a view."

Although he could still feel the tension bubbling just below the surface of their words, the fact that they were even speaking made him feel a little better.

Punctuating the seriousness of their situation, a large wave slammed into the side of the ship, causing it to list heavily to the right before it rocked slowly back to the left. Wet timbers creaked ominously. A loud voice cried out from somewhere near the front of the boat, and tightening his grip on the mast, Nick ducked his head beneath the sail to see what was happening.

The two-armed crew members were running for the bow. Squinting through the heavy sheets of rain, Nick saw a large beam on the mast at the very front of the ship swinging wildly from side to side. Obviously, something had gone wrong and the sailors were rushing to help.

The deck immediately below them was clear of Shades. They must have gone below. Considering their debility, they were probably leery of a rolling ship and a rain-slickened deck. But whatever the reason for their disappearance, it looked like now was a good time to climb down and find another place to hide before they were hit by lightning.

Nick forced a smile in Jo's direction. "Ladies first," he said.

Jo huffed softly. "Now, suddenly, you're a gentleman? Thanks a lot, Sir Lancelot," she muttered, but she scooted closer and began the climb down without another word of protest.

Once on the deck, they scurried like stiff, wet rats, crouching and dashing from one from meager shelter to the next. Neither one declaring themselves the leader, they worked their way mid-ship. "Over here," Jo hissed and headed towards what looked like a row of barrels covered with a large piece of canvas. Nick crawled under the cover, trying to ignore the needles stabbing his legs and feet as his circulation began to flow.

It was a relief to be protected from the driving rain and slashing wind. Squatting down beside Jo under the tarp, he gently maneuvered the canvas until a small hole was eye-level. Trying to suppress his cold shivering, Nick squinted through the small tear to scan the deck.

He spied a large wooden chest resting near the railing towards the bow of the ship. He frowned as he realized it must be the trunk that he and Jo had been locked in. Nudging Jo, he leaned back slightly to allow her a chance to peek out at the container. "Home sweet..." He froze as garbled voices moved towards them.

"Aye, she promises to be a rough 'en." Peeking cautiously through the hole, Nick's stomach tightened when a pair of one-armed sailors shuffled up the stairs and stopped in the shelter of the cabin.

"It be a bad omen," the one on the left growled.

Up close, it was even more obvious where the maimed crew had derived their name. Their skin was pale with no hint of veins, no blush of color. The eyes staring out into the storm were cloudy and lifeless. Their voices sounded as though they were being strained through a bag of stones... or bones.

"What mean ye? A bad omen?" Nick shuddered when the man on the right rubbed his festering, amputated limb over a row of sparse whiskers that sprouted along his bony jaw. The movement left a shiny smear of pus on his sunken face.

"First, there be stowaways who be disappearing like...like," the Shade shuffled to a stop. His mouth moved as if he were tasting words, trying to find the right one. "Like ghosts. Like shadows," he finally managed, sounding as damaged as he looked. "I saw 'em with me own eyes. Weren't it me who be finding 'em? Locked away they were." With spasmodic movements, he gestured with his stump towards the chest. "Then this wicked, cruel storm. Delaying us from the Keeper's time." He exchanged a haunted look with his companion and lowered his voice. "Mark me words, the Captain brings evil upon us."

"Yer own words be marking yer end," someone else barked, and with a fierce scowl, Mr. Amherst stepped from the shadows. Drawing a heavy knife from his belt, he placed the tip of the blade against the sunken chest of the Shade who'd made the unfortunate mistake of speaking ill of the Captain.

Nick's eyes widened as he watched the emaciated man shake his head, holding up his only hand in a placating manner. "Have mercy, sir."

The Bosun smiled. "Mercy?" he said, in a tone that suggested he'd never heard of the word.

Nick shuddered as the Shade's mouth dropped open in the now familiar death cry. The unholy noise was cut short by the knife which sank to the hilt in the skeletal ribcage. When the Bosun twisted the knife then pulled it free with a loud sucking noise, bile burned the back of Nick's throat.

Mr. Amherst wiped the blade of the knife on his filthy pants and glared at the Shade on the right, who stared back with dull eyes. "Have ye something to say?"

The Shade looked down at the crumpled corpse of his companion then gave an awkward shrug. "It be no matter."

"Right then." The Bosun smirked and nudged the body with his boot. "Get ye rid of that," he ordered, "then find ye the missing stowaways and bring 'em to me and me alone. Understood?"

All the while, a bloodied Whistler dangled at the Bosun's side. A silent witness, his tail curled up in a smug grin.

Nick sat back and closed his eyes, pressing his forehead against the wall of barrels. His imagination betrayed him, painting a vivid picture as he listened to the soft grunts and sliding sounds of a one-armed creature dragging another across the deck. The scene closed with a loud splash. He squeezed his eyes tightly closed and struggled against his heaving stomach. Finally, the shuffling footsteps faded.

"Are they gone?" Jo's breath tickled his ear as she strained to peer through their tiny window. "What's happening? I can't see anything."

He didn't want to answer. He couldn't. All he could do was lean heavily against a barrel and hug his knees, taking shaky gasps of salt-laden air through his mouth. He was grateful for his empty stomach. He was pretty sure the images of the knife stabbing into the bony chest and the blood, thinned by rainwater, flowing across the deck would haunt him forever.

Nick had no idea how long he sat there, resting his head on his knees. Much to his relief, Jo seemed content to rustle quietly through her backpack giving him time to pull his scattered emotions together.

He jumped when she tapped his cheek with a half empty bottle of water. "Need a drink?"

Nodding eagerly, he pressed the bottle to his lips, but he'd barely swallowed before he stopped and lowered it. Goosebumps forming on his skin, he whispered, "Something's wrong." He wasn't sure how he knew that, but suddenly getting a drink was no longer his top priority.

Jo blinked back at him. "What?"

Nick didn't bother to answer. He pressed his face to the hole in the canvas, moved it so that he could survey the ship. The deck was clear, but he couldn't shake the feeling that eyes were watching them, and he couldn't blot out the Bosun's unexpected appearance and the ruthless slaughter that followed. 'There are no rules here,' he thought, but he almost immediately amended it. 'There are rules, but I don't know what they are.'

He looked around cautiously, trying his best not to draw attention to their temporary hideaway. Finally, he tilted the canvas so that he could gaze up at the upper deck where the Captain's quarters sat like a coiled snake on a piece of driftwood.

Captain Samael leaned casually against the railing, an old-fashioned brass spyglass dangled loosely in one hand, but it was clear it wasn't the storm he had been studying. What little moisture Nick had managed to swallow evaporated. Frozen, overcome with dread, Nick watched as the Captain appeared to stare directly at him through the tiny rip in the fabric; he waited for the order that would herald their capture. But the Captain of the Shade Runner remained mute. His dark eyes seemed to feed on Nick, like a parasite nourished by fear alone.

"Hey," Jo smacked his arm lightly, "I think I see a rowboat on the other side of the ship. Maybe we can hide in there."

In the periphery of his vision, Nick saw her peering through another small tear, scrutinizing the path to the boat with a critical eye. "The cover is loose on the back. I can see it flapping. I think we can slip in and secure it so it doesn't draw attention. What do you think?"

Like a rabbit caught in a predator's gaze, Nick couldn't respond. He simply stared back into the cold dark eyes.

Aggravation colored Jo's voice when he ignored her. "At least it'd give us some protection, and maybe we could stretch out and get a little rest. Unless you've got a better idea." When he still didn't answer, she turned on him. "Are you listening to....What? What are you looking at?" She pressed one eye back against her peephole and followed Nick's line of sight. "Oh, crap."

The Captain's gaze shifted slightly as if capturing Jo and gloved fingers touched the wide brim of his hat as his head dipped once in a gentlemanly nod of acknowledgement. Her mouth hanging open, Jo lifted her hand as if she were going to wave back at him through the canvas, but then the Captain's lips twisted into a cruel grin. Without a sound, he turned and vanished into his cabin, leaving them shaken.

"We've got to get out of here," Nick announced. "Now. He may be sounding the alarm."

"Where to?" Jo gestured around them. "Ocean, Bosun, Shades, and oh yeah, storm, remember? That kind of cuts down on the possibilities."

Although his heart was racing, Nick felt numb, and he wondered if he was in shock. Like the lurching Shades, his vision stumbled over the deck as his brain wobbled its way towards a solution. "Below," he heard himself whisper and he looked at Jo. Her face was pale and her cheeks looked sunken. "We've got to go below."

Her eyes widened. "Down," she gulped, "the stairs?"

Nick nodded. "No choice. Besides, Mike's down there."

"Yeah, well," Jo looked towards the dark stairway, "so is most of the crew, especially the zombies."

"Look," Nick hesitated, afraid that his quivering voice would betray him, "I get it if you don't want to go. I don't either. No telling what's down there. Just thinking about it freaks me out. But," he felt his shoulders droop as his voice trailed off, "he's my dad."

Jo studied him with steady brown eyes then her thin shoulders lifted slightly. "Then, let's go."

Ticketless, they slipped into the darkened horror house of the Shade Runner Fair. Slinking down the rickety stairs, his back pressed against the damp wall, Nick felt like he was watching himself in a movie, the kind that he and his buddies had often watched from the safety of their theater seats. There, he'd mocked and jeered as loudly as his friends. But here, sneaking through a living nightmare where one-armed monsters lurked in the shadows, Nick found nothing to mock, nothing funny.

Feeling their way with their hands and feet, they reached the bottom of the stairs without encountering anyone and followed the wall around a sharp corner. Nick stopped when he stubbed his toe. Reaching out with tentative fingers, he studied the water-logged boards. They seemed to be in a small alcove or a closet without a door. Water dripped, echoing through a black, cavernous hollow. The sound stretched Nick's taut nerves even tighter as he unconsciously found the beat. 'Better...watch it. Better...watch it. Better... watch it,' the droplets warned.

Squinting into the noxious gloom, Nick grimaced as small shadows darted along the top of the wall, just inches from their heads. "Rats!" he warned.

"Oh, that's just great!" Jo whispered and stepped close to him. Pressing herself against his back and sounding far younger and less confident than she had topside, she added, "Did I mention that I really, really hate rats?"

It seemed natural to turn to find her hand in the dark. Unfortunately, he didn't see the low shelf that banged his shins and drove him to his knees with a muffled grunt.

"Are you okay?" Jo's frightened voice seemed to magnify in the dark, even though he knew she was speaking in a soft hush. "You didn't get bit, did you?"

"No, no. I'm fi-" He was pushing himself to his feet when he heard a familiar, awkward shuffling noise off to their right. He scanned the darkness for its source, but it was impossible to see anything in the murkiness. Without stopping to think, Nick grabbed Jo's hand and yanked her down beside him.

"What are you doing?" she demanded.

He pressed his lips against her ear. "Someone's out there. Close." Squatting in the dark, they listened as the shambling footsteps drew closer. Nick could feel each rabid beat of his heart against the back side of his chest. The reverberation of his breathing was deafening. "Get ready to run," he murmured into Jo's ear. "Keep low and follow me."

"Skins," a low voice hissed. Nearby, something dragged across wet planks. Maybe a sack of potatoes, if they were lucky, but more likely the foot of a one-armed zombie. "I smell you, Skins. I know you be close."

Nick caught the whiff of truth behind the predator's statement as he was nearly overcome by a putrid stench. He didn't dare lift a hand to pinch his nostrils closed. Instead, he breathed shallowly through his mouth and tried not to gag at the rotten, dead smell.

"You be mine, Skins."

Nick's eyes sawed uselessly back and forth, cutting a blind path through their inky surroundings like a butter knife trying to slice through a slab of onyx. He felt a shiver course through Jo's hand then her entire body tensed. Just when he felt that the anxiety would reach out its only hand to choke him with bony fingers, three shrill notes from somewhere above pierced the pitch darkness. Through the ebony mist, a shadowy figure appeared, cocking its skeletal head towards the sound.

"Ready the Runner for the blow!" the Bosun's voice bellowed down the stairwell. "All hands to the foredeck!"

Immediately, the murky hold was filled with a graceless shuffling and an overpowering scent that sent tremors up Nick's spine. He watched as one emaciated shadow after another arose from the darkness and moved towards the rectangle of dim light above.

"Shades," Jo whispered needlessly as the silent parade passed. Nick swallowed hard, thinking how easily they could have stumbled into a roomful of waiting, bony arms. As the last of the crew lurched up the stairs, Nick staggered to his feet.

He stood there trying to decide whether the swaying was because of his shaking or because of the storm. The heavy weight of indecision pinned him to the floor despite the rolling of the Shade Runner. He was surrounded by a great darkness — the belly of the ship, a deadly storm, an unknown ocean, a strange world. The situation felt vast and hopeless. Dripping water reiterated its unnecessary warning. Otherwise, there was silence. No crew, no guards, no prisoners.

No Mike.

"I thought it'd be easy to find him."

"Over here," Jo called softly. Unaware she'd stepped away from him, Nick followed her voice, stumbling like a Shade towards her in the dark. "You can bet those guys will be back," she said, "and we'd better have a good hiding place when they do. Then we can worry about finding your dad."

Nick strained to see down the narrow hallway Jo had found. "Whoa, creepy."

"Yeah, well look around. This isn't exactly the Hilton. Hang on a minute," Jo ordered. He could barely see her digging around in her backpack then, suddenly, the blackness was split by a narrow beam of light. It took a second for his eyes to adjust to the change, but when they did, he saw Jo holding up a small flashlight.

"Are you a Boy Scout?"

She grinned lopsidedly. "Let's go," she said.

Shaking his head, Nick followed the light. Fighting claustrophobia, he moved cautiously down the hall. It seemed to be some sort of storage area. They skirted heavy barrels and clambered over stacked wooden boxes. They might be able to barricade themselves in if they had to. It probably wouldn't stop those guys, but it would slow them down. There didn't seem to be another way out.

Finally, they reached what appeared to be a dead end. Ignoring the bite of the rough wood against his back, Nick slid to the floor. Drawing his knees tightly against his chest, he bowed his head. He couldn't hear wind or thunder, but it was obvious from the violent swaying of the ship that the storm was gathering momentum.

Nick didn't bother to look up when Jo dropped next to him and grunted softly, "So what now?"

The bowels of the Shade Runner groaned out a litany of Nick's failures. He silently counted the number of times the ship rolled from side to side. He reached fourteen before finally admitting, "I don't know."

He waited for a biting retort or some slightly scandalous name-calling, but the only sounds were those of the sea pummeling the wooden hull, calling out promises that all ended in a watery death. Listening to the threats, Nick sucked in a wobbly breath of stale, salty air and turned his back to Jo. He pressed his face against the wall then reached up a hand to steady himself when the ship heaved. "I don't know what to do, Dad," he whispered, low enough that Jo wouldn't hear.

He was unaware of the warm tears that slid down his cheeks and dropped to the wet floor. They were consumed by the belly of the ship.

CHAPTER 9

THE BEAST OF BERKEN BAY

"Nick?"

He only knew he'd dozed when Jo's whisper awakened him. For a moment, he didn't move, didn't respond. He simply sat there, curled up against the wall. He was reluctant to pull his face and hand from the boards. It was his only contact with something solid, the only touch of reality in an otherwise unreal situation. For all he knew, Mike was just on the other side of the wall, inches that may as well have been a hundred thousand miles away.

"I think I hear something," Jo whispered, even softer than before.

He perked up at that, sitting up straight. Like the ship, he strained, putting everything he had left within him into hearing whatever it was Jo was hearing. The sound, when he finally caught it, was faint. It gyrated with the wild movement of the ship — rising when the waves sucked away from the sides of the boat and the Shade Runner sank into the furrows of the sea; ebbing when the violent storm tides rammed into the creaking timbers lifting the ship onto the crest of the ocean. Behind it all and from somewhere above them, the faint cries of the crew painted a backdrop, setting the scene.

"Do you–"

Nick shushed her. His tired voice sounded harsher than he'd intended. He touched her knee and gave a single nod. He'd been on the brink of understanding what he was hearing when she'd spoken. He pressed his ear to the wall again. The sound took on momentum. He listened for a moment before leaning close to Jo.

"A rustling sound?"

Her expression was unreadable in the dim light, but panic tinged her voice. "You don't think it's rats, do you?"

The ship heaved violently and a crazy sprig of Jo's hair sprang free of its braid. He immediately thought of frizzy-haired Miriam. The Watcher had told him that he would learn hard things, like what it was like to leave someone behind. Nick silently vowed that he'd go to a watery death before he left without Mike then he hoped that if the time came, he'd have the courage to follow through with his promise.

Miriam had also warned him about Dark Watchers. Despite all the time they'd spent locked in the trunk and hiding on the mast, he hadn't really taken time to ponder her grim warning. He'd been too busy trying to survive. Now, hearing the muffled noises coming through the wall, he wondered if perhaps some nasty version of Miriam was peeking back at him through a crack in the boards. He pulled his face away from the wall just in case.

"Seems like it'd take an awful lot of rats to make that much noise," Jo worried aloud.

"I don't think it's rats. It sounds like...people. Moving around."

"The prisoners?" Jo said.

"Ye be right, lass," a deep voice quietly affirmed.

Nick and Jo both jumped, startled at the nearness of the strange voice. Bumping into one another, they scrambled to get away from whoever had followed them to their hiding place. Unexpectedly slamming his right shoulder into a wall he couldn't see, Nick's flesh prickled in anticipation of the cold, deathly grip of a hand around his ankle or his arm. Or maybe the man would simply grab him around the throat and throttle him before he could cry out a warning to Jo.

Was it one of the crew or one of the zombies? And if he had to choose, which would be worse? 'Zombies,' he silently answered and instinctively ducked his head to protect his neck. But nothing happened, and the corridor remained a dead end.

Dead end? How appropriate. The term had never seemed ominous before, but he'd never use it the same way ever again. At least, not if he got out of this particular dead end alive.

Jo was gasping, a panicked gulping sound, and Nick figured he sounded just about as brave as she did. Trying not to touch anything too personal or private, he managed to turn around and press his back against Jo in a feeble effort to shield her.

"Are ye daft?" their pursuer hissed. "Be ye quiet unless ye want us all to die!"

His pulse banged incessantly, deafeningly, against his temples. Nick started to ask the man who he was, but before he could speak, his question was answered in a hushed baritone.

"Me name be Angus. Angus Dent of Berken Bay. Used to be anyways," he softly added. "Ye scared me witless, ye did."

Feeling Jo relax her firm grip on the back of his shirt, Nick eased away from her and squinted into the darkness. He could barely make out a lank shadow. "What are you, Mr. Dent?" he whispered, meaning Shade or crew.

There was a hesitation before the man answered, "I be a dead man."

'Shade,' Nick thought and felt himself gasp and pull back from the creature in front of him.

"No, lad. Ye miss my meaning." The shadow scuttled closer then two strong hands were clutching his shoulders. Two hands! "I be whole yet. I still be a man, I swear by the Scribe that will soon be the death of me."

"What are you talking about?" Jo said.

"Not here," Angus Dent said and grabbed Nick's hand. He wrapped Nick's fingers around his right arm. "Follow me," he ordered and took off.

He led them on a twisting path through a warren of narrow corridors and hatchways that seemed too small to have ever been intended for a grown man. Feeling like a blind man in a labyrinth, Nick clamped desperate fingers into Dent's skinny bicep while Jo held onto the tail of Nick's shirt with both hands. The only sounds of their passing were the soft shuffle of his and Jo's shoes on the smooth boards and the occasional thump of the backpack against the constricted passageways. Nick wondered why the man seemed unconcerned about the noises they were making then he realized that they sounded just like rats scurrying through the bowels of the Shade Runner.

Finally, they stepped through a doorway onto a sharply sloped floor. Angus Dent immediately slowed his pace. Nick was glad since both he and Jo were stumbling and feeling their way with their sneakered feet over large timbers that rose up like storm waves in front of them. Their leader came to an abrupt stop.

"We be safe here," Angus said, his voice echoing in what felt like a vast space. Nick's eyes growing accustomed to the dark, he saw the vague form of a man settle down between two large beams.

Keeping himself between the stranger and the doorway leading back into the ship, Nick squatted down a few feet away. Jo knelt beside him and studied the face of their guide intently.

"I'm Jo, Mr. Dent," she said. "Jo Torres."

"It be a pleasure...considering." Angus cocked his head toward Nick. "And ye, young man? What be yer name?"

He hesitated to give the man any information, but he supposed it couldn't hurt. "Nick Sanchez." He stared at the man's drawn face. "Have you ever heard of someone named Fidel? Fidel Sanchez?"

Angus appeared to think about it then shook his head. "No. Should I be knowing him?"

Nick shrugged. "Probably not. It was just a long shot. But, you could tell us everything you know about this place." He flinched at the bony elbow that was suddenly planted in his ribs, but Angus Dent was wiping a trembling hand over his face and didn't seem to notice.

Her face smudged with grime and chocolate, Jo gave him a dirty look before digging around in her backpack. "Are you hungry, Mr. Dent? Thirsty?"

"Oh, lass. Don't ye be beguiling an old man on his last legs."

Nick and Jo exchanged a confused shrug. "I have some water." Jo passed him a plastic bottle. Mr. Dent held it up, studied it, jostled it, then frowned over at them. "Here," Jo said, and reached over and popped up the plastic cap.

Dent took a tentative sip then, apparently getting the hang of the sport bottle, he tilted it up and swallowed several large gulps before lowering the bottle, wiping an arm across his mouth, and sighing loudly. Before he could speak, Jo passed him an apple. "It's kind of bruised. Sorry."

Angus bit into the fruit and chewed like a man who hadn't eaten in days. He soon finished off the apple, core and all, and washed it down with the last of the water. He leaned back against the curved sides of the boat, giving them a glance colored by a blush on his filthy cheeks.

"Now I've gone and done it," he said. "I've had the last of yer food and water without even offering ye any of it ye own selves."

"Oh, no," Jo said, "we have—"

"We just ate," Nick said, interrupting her. 'Don't let him know we have more food,' he warned her with a frown. Whether she understood his meaning or not, Jo gave him a hesitant nod, and Nick turned his attention back to the stranger. "Mr. Dent, what did you mean about being a dead man, but still being whole?"

Angus considered them for a long moment then settled himself into the gap between the beams. "Where ye be from that ye don't know the Shade Runner and its workings?"

Nick grabbed Jo's arm, but stared at Dent. No way should they answer that question.

Finally, Angus gave a gap-toothed smile. "Well, I guess it don't be my concern, so long as ye ain't Travelers. And I suppose by now that the good citizens of Tempest and all of Susskipo knows they ain't no such thing. It be a myth is all. A horrible myth."

"What be a myth, Mr. Dent?" Jo said.

"Why, this." He pulled a tattered piece of paper from where it had been tucked inside his shirt.

Nick took it and squinted at it in the meager light. "I can't make it out, but it looks like the same notice I saw posted in town."

"Aye, lad. Posted everywhere, they is. And no need reading it, they always say the same thing. Only the name of the town be changing." Mr. Dent straightened and cocked his head, speaking with a melodramatic lilt. "From the Keeper with respect to the Gathering of the Shades. Ye be remiss, and I am forced to impose harsher Rules of Business. As if the Rules of Business could be any harsher," he added in a whisper before continuing. "Tis not my fault. It is ye who are negligent. Bring me a Traveler. Line the pockets of yer favorite local crimp. If'n you have one," he directed at Jo with a wink. He turned to Nick. "Increase the fleet, lad, and win a miserly amount that ain't worth the pocket it be carried in."

Angus pointed a finger at Nick as if it were a sword. "Bring me a Traveler!"

Nick gulped as Jo's hand squeezed his arm.

"But, why?" Nick said, handing the paper back to its owner. "Why does the Keeper want me-," he stopped. "I mean, why does he want a Traveler so badly?"

"And what is a Traveler exactly?" Jo added.

Angus frowned at them as he settled back in his cramped nest between the beams. "Ye truly do be strangers," he murmured. "Well, I'll tell ye, the Keeper be needing a Traveler only so's he can travel the Bridge his own self. Because he hungers for power like a dindle-beast hungers for gruel."

"Travel the Bridge?" Jo frowned.

Mr. Dent sighed. "Tis said there be an invisible bridge that stretches between this world and another."

"The Einstein-Rosen Bridge," Nick whispered.

It was Dent's turn to frown then he shook his head. "I be not educated in the particulars, lad. I repeat only what I's been told since the first days of the Gathering."

"So the Keeper wants a Traveler to take him to the Bridge?" Nick said.

"No. He does not *want* a Traveler. He *must* have one or he cannot cross the Bridge. The legend says he tried it to no avail when the cube first fell into his evil hands."

"What's a cube?" Jo said.

Dent smiled. "Well, it be not a cube for one thing."

Nick rubbed a hand over his face. He was tired and the old man's talk was confusing.

"It be a key," Angus continued. "The story goes that only the Keeper and a single trusted servant have ever laid eyes on it. But I be hearing that the cube, or the key, looks like neither." He glanced around then leaned towards them. "My sources be saying that, in fact, it be looking somewhat like a coin."

Nick perked up, his eyes widening to take in Angus Dent's shadowy form. "A coin?"

"Aye," Mr. Dent nodded. "Passage for the bridge, ye see. But, there be the rub." He leaned back again. "For there be no Bridge."

"Are you sure?" Jo said with a sideways smirk at Nick.

Mr. Dent's voice turned nasty, hate-filled. "The whole sorry thing be the product of the Scribe." He shook the paper in his hand. "The author of this."

"The Scribe?"

His eyes filling with unshed tears that glistened in the dim light, Dent met Nick's gaze. "If there be a hell, the Scribe be the Keeper of it." He cleared his throat. "He be the reason the soulless ones raise the sails and ride the seas."

"The Shades," Nick muttered.

"Aye, lad. The Shades." Angus Dent raised one shaky hand, studying the calloused palm, the dirty, ragged fingernails that were shaped like tiny shovels. "And I be joining them soon. Shortly after we spy land, I fear."

"Why?" Jo sounded on the verge of tears and the single word slipped out like a plea.

Mr. Dent lowered his hand, cradling it in his lap like a treasured pet. "Because I be gathered, child, and I reckon I cannot hide from them for long. And when me hand fails to turn the key to the Bridge — and fail it will since it be a myth — the Keeper in his anger be taking that hand." He gave a crooked, humorless grin. "And me soul along with it."

Nick's head filled with white noise as his brain churned to comprehend the prisoner's words. He struggled to accept the fact that if Mr. Dent, who'd been kidnapped or 'gathered,' was going to lose a hand and soul to the Keeper, Mike was headed for the same cruel fate. Ragged breaths escaped between his clenched teeth as one thought pummeled him unmercifully. His dad would be one of the walking dead if something wasn't done. But, what could be done? The Bosun had the coin — the cube — the key. And there was no other way out. Unless…

"Mr. Dent, what if the Keeper were to find a Traveler? A real one?"

It took a moment before Angus seemed to hear the question then he blinked and stared at Nick. "If the tale be true, ye mean?" At Nick's nod, the old man made a noise that could have been a moan or a muffled protest. "Then we all be doomed to hell. The evil the Keeper be bringing on Susskipo, he be taking o'er the Bridge with him. And do ye honestly think he be satisfied with one more world? No. He be wanting more and more. And woe to the poor Traveler that be falling in his grasp. Only Eli can save him."

Jo frowned. "Who's Eli?"

"Why, the One, of course. The Maker," Dent replied.

"The Shades," Nick said, thinking about Mike and not about some One named Eli. "Isn't there some way to save them?"

Angus stared back at him. "Aye," he finally admitted. "Death."

"No," he protested aloud, "there has to be some other way."

The old man shook his head. "I be not knowing how he does it, Nick Sanchez, but when the Keeper takes the hand, the soul be going with it. Did ye not see the stages of the Shades?"

"Stages?" Jo said. "What do you mean?"

"Did ye not see that some be further across the divide, be more creature and less man than others?" Now that he mentioned it, Nick had noticed that some of them were more gaunt, more glazed than the others. "The longer they be Shades, the less human they be. At the end, they cannot even be understanding what is said to them, or recognizing kinfolk. Then," Angus shuddered, "they be carried off to the mines or tossed to the sharks."

They were all silent for a few minutes. The only sounds were those of the muffled waves, the creaking of the timbers, and the scurrying of the rats. The only movement was the ship's constant swaying.

"Do you have a family?" Jo finally whispered, and this time she really was crying.

"Yes, child. Me blessed wife, Maidre, and me three sons. Me boys be grown now and having children of their own. They be taking right good care of their momma now, I reckon," he said, nodding. He looked down at his well-used hands. "If ye young 'uns be escaping the Shade Runner and if ye find yerselves near Berken Bay, look up me family, would ye? They be living in the white cottage on the Valley Green outside Berken Bay. Tell 'em, tell 'em..."

Jo scooted nearer to the old man and rested a hand on his knee. "We'll tell them you love them, Mr. Dent, and that your thoughts were of them." Dent smiled and patted her hand.

"No," Nick said, and the other two gave him puzzled looks. He squirmed under their eyes. "We're not doing that. You two are talking like he's dead, and he ain't."

"Not yet, lad, but soon," Angus said.

Nick shook his head. He couldn't believe that. He wouldn't. Because if he did, that meant Mike was facing the same fate. There had to be something that could be done. The only solution was the coin. So, he'd just have to find the Bosun and take it back.

He steeled himself against Angus Dent's sad face. "Look, my dad's one of the prisoners on this rotting boat. That's why we're here. We have to find him, and you have to help us. Then, we're all getting out of here."

Mr. Dent didn't even answer, he simply stared back.

"There's no other way," Nick insisted.

Angus studied them both then forced a weary smile. "I reckon we shall fail, but I reckon we must try." Nick gave the old man a nod. "Besides, it'll give ye a chance to take yer leave of yer father."

Nick didn't argue, instead he tossed Jo her backpack and stood as Mr. Dent pushed himself to his unsteady feet with a groan.

"I guess we be getting back in the same way I got me own self out," Angus announced and led them toward the warren of narrow corridors and tiny doorways.

"Mr. Dent," Jo said as they picked their way across the large timbers to the rolling of the ship, "what's a crimp?"

Angus didn't pause as he looked at them over his left shoulder. "Why, a crimp be a scoundrel, lass. A no good scamp who be selling his own mother just to line his pocket. They cannot be trusted," he said. "Do not be believing anything a crimp says. Steer clear of them entirely 'less you have a hankering to meet the Keeper and the Scribe." He looked in front of him just in time to avoid tripping over a rotten beam. "I ought to know, having been one me own self. Now, come along, children."

CHAPTER 10

RECONNECTING THE DOTS

"Watch yer step, this wee hop be a shortcut to the brig."

Even as his exhausted brain made a feeble attempt to unravel the whispered warning, Nick lost his footing. One minute he was rushing to keep up with Angus Dent's wasted figure, and the next, the floor disappeared beneath his feet. He pitched forward like a drunken man stepping off a ledge, fighting in vain to right himself. His arms flailed madly and for one long, sickening moment, Nick felt his body fall into oblivion.

A single weary thought dominated his mind: The old man had lied.

Angus had led them to a watery death that in terms of fright was second only to death at the hands — no pun intended — of the Shades. As Nick waited for the cold waves to swallow him, gravity fashioned of regrets and failures pulled him down through a rush of timelessness. But rather than waves, it was the solid floor of the Shade Runner that stopped his fall.

The loud grunt that punctuated his landing had barely escaped his lips when he was flattened by Jo's equally ungraceful swan dive.

"Be ye deaf? T'was fair warning I be giving ye." Nick craned his neck. In the dim light, he could see Angus's skinny arms resting on his bony hips as he viewed the perplexing tangle just one deep step from his bare feet. "Now, stop ye child's play. Time be short."

Angus Dent thought this was child's play? The very thought that Nick and Jo were doing this for fun brought Nick as close to laughter as he'd been in a very long time. And maybe he would have laughed if he wasn't exhausted and hungry and scared and battling hopelessness. But he was all those things, so the humorous urge passed quickly until more than anything, he just wanted to lay there. He wanted to collapse like tire-marked roadkill onto the deck, his cheek pressed into the rough boards, his limp body bobbing on the surface of a storm-tossed ocean. He started to lower his head, give in to the notion, but a flicker of conscience reminded him that Mike and Jo were stuck here because of him. He didn't have the right to give up, not until he fixed this mess he'd created.

When Jo rolled off him and lay panting on the planks, Nick climbed stiffly to his feet, unable to stifle a groan. "You okay?" he said and reached down a hand to her.

She nodded, got to her feet, and began brushing off her jeans. Her hands slowed then froze. She looked up at him and gave him a crooked grin. "Habit," she said, her voice quivering. "I guess a little more dirt isn't going to make much difference, is it?" She tucked a stray lock of hair behind her ear.

"No, not much," Nick agreed, as he stared absently at her grimy clothes and smudged face. He flicked a grin back at her, a half-hearted attempt that probably looked more like a grimace. His face hardened as he was reminded of another filthy 'friend,' a boy who prowled the dusty streets of Tempest. He turned to face Angus. "Mr. Dent, what's redemption?"

The man's face blanched and his eyes shifted as if even the walls were listening. The ship lurched like a Shade on a particularly wicked wave and somewhere far above them, thunder rumbled a low-throated warning. "That's not to be spoke of, lad!" Angus croaked in a fierce whisper.

Arms and legs shaking with exhaustion, Nick hauled himself up to the deck on which Angus stood then pulled Jo up behind him before facing the self-named ex-crimp. "Simon, the boy who brought us here, talked about it just before we boarded. To the Bosun. It sounded like they were making some sort of deal."

"And so they likely be." Swaying with the rocking of the ship, Angus licked his thin lips then lowered his voice even further until Nick had to strain to hear him. "Redemption be yet another myth. One that some be clinging to, and a nasty transaction it be for all involved." He looked at Nick with something like pity. "For those believing in it, it be their only hope to be getting back a stolen loved one. An exchange, ye might say."

"What kind of exchange?" The trepidation in his voice was gravelly as the question scraped across his dry vocal chords.

"Why, one life for another, lad. A man whole traded for one of the maimed and soulless."

"But," nausea and something else — was it hate? — twisted in Nick's gut, "Simon saved my life."

"Perhaps." Angus studied Nick and Jo, his dull eyes sweeping them up and down as if he'd just now laid eyes on them. "But, perhaps, he merely saved ye to trade ye."

Nick opened his mouth to reply, to deny it, but no words came out.

"Look, lad," Angus stepped closer, but still it was hard to hear him over the sounds of the storm, "ye musn't hold it too much against him. Likely this Simon ye speak of has someone onboard. A brother perchance, or a father. If I be guessing, I be saying he turned ye over in the hopes of gaining back some poor lost soul aboard this very Shade Runner. But, pity yer friend, for there be no release once the hand be taken. Redemption," he turned his head and spat, "it be nothing but another in the Scribe's web of lies."

Nick stared at the dark, wet splatter at his feet. The truth hammered at him with each pounding of his heart as the pieces fell into place. The look of loss on Simon's face when Nick had disappeared; the cry of desperation echoing throughout the courtyard as Nick had escaped back to Colorado Springs.

Simon had betrayed him. Led him here, sold him, and walked away. And Angus thought Nick should pity him? What about himself? After all, Nick hadn't enticed someone to this ratty old ship where death by Shade or shark awaited. Well, not if you didn't count, Jo. Why should he pity Simon? Why had he ever been concerned about whether Elliard was going to kill the filthy kid? Simon was nothing but a crimp in the making. Nick was right to feel nothing but hate for him.

Shoving his conflicting thoughts aside, he demanded, "Where's my dad?"

Anxiety etched a worried map across Angus's pallid features. "Be ye daft? Lower yer voice!" he whispered, searching the area with darting eyes. "The Shades be powerful good at making use of the gloom." He nodded towards a stack of crates outlined against a shadowy space a few yards from where they stood. "A pair of the buggers be laying low just there a few hours past."

"What were they doing?" The whites of Jo's eyes stood in stark relief to their murky surroundings. "Are they gone?"

"Ye be safe for now, lass." Angus assured her, and for the briefest of moments, Nick saw a hint of compassion in the old man's eyes. "As to why they be there," he shrugged a bony shoulder. "Who can say? Maybe they be searching for the two of ye, maybe they be hunting ol' Angus, or chasing rats. Maybe they be hiding their ownselves from the Captain's wrath, or that of the mate and his helper. But they be gone now, thank the Maker. That be all that matters."

"It's not all that matters," Nick muttered.

Angus silently glared at Nick, sizing him up, before pointing a calloused finger towards a narrow archway just beyond the crates. "The door to the makeshift brig be that way. I reckon I spied a man amongst us who be dressed and talking like ye. Ye be finding him down there with the rest."

Nick stared at the dirty finger then at the doorway it pointed to. The entrance to the hallway yawned open like the jaws of a shark — dark, painful, deadly. His stomach churned, his heart beat furiously inside his chest, and his mouth went as dry as three-week old bread. "You're not coming with us," he said, feeling as if he were being dragged down in a riptide — not wanting to stay or go, not trusting his senses, but having no choice in the matter. He was simply floundering.

"We be arriving at Bridge End soon," Angus announced. "I reckon I must plot me own escape. Even with nil of a chance of success for me poor self."

Reluctantly, Nick nodded. "The door to the brig." He had to swallow hard to steady his voice. "Is it locked?"

Angus's face softened into a ragged smile. "It be not much of a cell if it be not locked, now would it? Do ye leave yer brigs unlocked where ye call home then?"

Nick flushed at the sarcasm. "No, I don't guess so," he mumbled. "I've never seen one up close."

The old man's smile faded. "I reckon ye haven't, lad. It be easy to see, even in this poor light, that ye two be not belonging here."

Nick gave a noncommittal shrug and Jo nodded.

"Colorado Springs is different, Mr. Dent," Jo smiled weakly. "We don't have Shades or a Scribe or—" She stopped when Angus held up a dirty palm.

"Do not be telling me such things, child. I have no business knowing about a place such as that," he warned. "Even to dream of a place with no Shades, no Scribe…." Angus shook his head in weary fashion. "It be more than I can bear." Tired eyes glazed over and the wrinkled jaw hardened. For the first time, the crimp in Angus Dent shone through. "Now, ye best be gone. I have no wish to repay yer kindnesses with that which comes natural to my treacherous nature."

"But, people change, Mr. Dent." There was unmistakable confidence in Jo's voice. For a brief moment, even Nick believed her, and he wondered if she spoke from experience or from faith alone.

Disbelief and hope, good and evil, wrestled on the wrinkled battlefield of the old man's face. Finally, he nodded and gave Jo a strained smile. "Then it is that hope which shall keep us all alive, lass." Straightening his shoulders, Angus turned to Nick. "Aye, the door will be locked, but ye be having no trouble as the key hangs near."

"What about the chains?" Nick said. "They had the prisoners chained together and—"

"Up on deck?" Angus interrupted. Nick nodded. "I thought as much. There be no need for chains in the cell. The chain's purpose be not to prevent escape from the brig, but escape of a different nature, sure enough."

Nick frowned at the cryptic words. "What do you mean?"

Angus hesitated before replying. "It keeps weary souls from jumping o'er the rails into death's cold embrace."

"You mean it stops the prisoners from killing themselves?" Silence screamed the answer to Jo's question, and filled the dark corridors with an ugly truth.

"Once aboard the Shade Runner, the trap be closed. As I told ye, the only rescue for the soulless be death. But along with their hand, the Keeper steals the will, so that even with the opportunity a Shade will cling to his sorry life. Else, they'd fling themselves to the waves at first sail."

When Jo and Nick merely stared at him, Angus sighed. "Take me own pitiful self. Where am I to go? I hide, but they know I be aboard. So, they simply wait and watch 'til I tire of this wretched game. In the end, we prisoners be left to the mercy of the ocean or the Scribe, and I know which I will choose. Those that sail the Shade Runner — the whole and the dead — they know it, too. So, they protect the cargo, this," he gestured towards the hall which led to the cell, "this pitiful harvest of souls. There be nary a Traveler among them, yet the Keeper and the Scribe — curse them both — await."

"No," Nick snapped. "I don't believe that. I won't!" He grabbed Jo's wrist and crossed in front of the crates. Pulling her with him, he took a step into the dark maw of the hallway before glaring back at the old man. "I'm going to find my dad, Mr. Dent, and then I'm going to get us out of this mess. I'm not sure how, but I'll do it. If you don't want to come, well, then don't. You're crazy. Besides, you said yourself we shouldn't trust you. You're nothing but a crimp."

"Nick," Jo protested.

But Angus didn't deny it; he merely pointed his chin in the direction of the brig. "Be ye gone then. And be ye going with the Maker."

Nick tugged on Jo. "Come on. Let's go. We're better off without him."

The two walked away, and only Jo looked back at the silhouette of a broken man.

The corridor quickly swallowed them, narrowing like a funnel as they moved deeper into the ship's belly. Just when he felt the walls closing in on him, Nick found himself face to face with a thick door. The narrowness of the hallway left little room to maneuver, which he supposed helped to keep the prisoners under control. Otherwise, it was just as Angus Dent had described it, unguarded and — Nick put one hand on the door's iron handle and tried to move it — locked. A tiny barred window was cut high on the door.

"Give me a hand up," Jo ordered. When he questioned her with a look, she added. "Maybe I can spot Dr. Sanchez."

Without a word, Nick cupped his hands and hefted Jo up to the window. "See anything?" he grunted.

"They're in there," Jo whispered excitedly. "At least, there's somebody in there."

"Mike?"

She shook her head. "I can't make out their faces, but there's a bunch of people sitting and laying around in there, so..."

"There's a pretty good chance he's in there," Nick finished.

"Yeah." Jo hopped down and looked at him expectantly. "The key?"

Nick pointed to the peg protruding from the wall just out of reach of the window. It bore a rusty key secured to a leather thong.

"I knew Mr. Dent wasn't lying to us," Jo muttered.

"Uh-huh." Nick gave her a warning glare, hoping she'd let the subject drop, as he snagged the key and inserted it into the lock. "You stay here and stand guard. If someone comes, there's no chance if they lock us in. I'll find Mike."

"What? Why?" Jo looked scared, and in that moment, Nick thought about what it would be like to be left alone in a dark hallway where real monsters lurked. As he pushed open the door and stepped over the threshold, he reached out and grabbed her hand.

"If someone comes, if you hear anything, anything at all, don't wait around. Take off and go find Mr. Dent. Understand? I may not trust him, but he's all we've got."

Jo nodded, her eyes as big and as shiny as brand new quarters.

Nick stepped into the cell and, against his better judg-ment, leaned back against the door, closing it. He was immediately punched in the nose by the smell of pee and something else that he thought might be a mix of fear and despair. Except for the pee stink, he'd probably blend right in. Breathing through his mouth, he scanned the pinched faces that turned to squint up at him with haunted eyes. It was uncomfortable being center stage in front of a mute audience.

Nick straightened and his eyes shifted across row after row of men sitting or lying on the floor in various poses. Some were hunched, some twitched nervously, some already resembled Shades with their lifeless eyes and sunken cheeks. One man to the right was carrying on a rapid, non-stop monologue about a place called Levelard, or maybe he was talking about leveling a yard. There was even a man in the back pacing back and forth in a tiny corner — two steps, turn, two steps, turn. They all had one thing in common: they looked like busted toy soldiers, broken figures, no weapons in sight.

His heart fluttering wildly, Nick stepped away from the safety of the door and began to pick his way through the prisoners littering the floor. He stopped when he spied the large man who had dragged Mike down when they were up on deck. Now, the stranger lay in a forgotten heap in the middle of the floor. His pants were soiled and stained, and

Nick couldn't tell if he was dead or alive. He couldn't see the man's face, but his chest didn't seem to be moving. Turning his face away, Nick squeezed his eyes closed until he could get his breathing under control.

When he opened them, he tasted bitter anxiety rising in the back of his throat. Had Mike met the same fate on the stairway? Was he dead? Beaten to death in a damp and rotting prison? Would Nick have to go home without him? Leave him here in this strange world? Unburied. Simply gone like his grandfather, Fidel.

Nick's feet were leaden as he shuffled deeper into the whirlpool of doomed men.

"Nicco?"

Nick's heart stopped at the cracked whisper, and for the first time in his life, he was happy to hear the dreaded nickname. His eyes sought out a figure slumped in the corner to his right. Ignoring the grunts and curses of the men he trampled, Nick stumbled forward. Dropping to his knees, he reached out to touch his dad only to drop his hand a hair's breadth from making contact.

"Is it really you?" Mike stretched out a dirty hand and tentatively touched Nick's face. He shook his head. "Nicco, you shouldn't be here."

Nick forced a cocky grin. "I could say the same thing about you."

His dad hesitated then shrugged awkwardly. "Okay, I'll concede that point."

"Are you okay?" He hadn't missed the fact that a simple shrug had caused his dad to wince as if in pain.

"I fell a bit. Coming down the stairs."

Nick didn't mention that he'd seen that. Instead, he simply said, "We need to go." He gazed at the blood-splattered rag that had once been his father's favorite shirt and swallowed hard. "Can you walk?"

Mike glanced down at himself. "It isn't mine, Nicco. The blood isn't mine. Most of it anyway. I saw a man get—I..."

When he didn't say anything else, Nick added, "You can lean on me, if you need to." He stuck out his hand and was pleased to feel that Mike's grip, when he latched onto him, was strong and trembled only slightly.

Mike struggled unsteadily to his feet. "Made it," he hissed between clenched teeth. When Nick eyed him warily, he said, "I'm a bit stiff is all. And have a slight headache," he admitted.

Nick nodded, eyeing the ugly bruise where the heavy club had struck Mike when he'd first been taken in the alley behind the store. "Jo's waiting outside the door," he whispered as he looked intently at the other prisoners.

A few stared back at him with a desperation so intense that Nick suddenly realized the absolute truth in Angus Dent's grim words. These men probably considered the dead man sprawled on the floor the lucky one. They would welcome death rather than a future of soulless service to the Keeper and the Scribe. A sudden thought made Nick frown: Would any of these men try to bargain for their freedom with a piece of information gained through eavesdropping?

"Jo? Rosa's daughter? What's she..."

"Not now," Nick warned, his voice low as he urged Mike towards the door. "I'll explain later. Right now, we have to get out of here."

It seemed to take forever to cross the small room. The task of stepping over and around the prisoners was multiplied by Mike's stumbling gait, but mostly by the unpredictable and violent listing of the Shade Runner. Somewhere near them, a prisoner groaned and vomited again and again. Nick could only be grateful that seasickness had thus far bypassed both he and Jo. Above their heads, somewhere beyond the low ceiling, thunder snapped and rolled to the tune of a shrill howling that was not unlike the screeching of the Shades. It had to be wind, Nick thought, and he wondered if the ship and the storm had finally collided, or if worse was yet to come. Thoughts as dark as the fathomless water lapping a few inches beneath his feet were hard to hold at bay. Keeping one outstretched hand on the rough boards of the wall for support and the other wrapped around Mike's clammy hand, Nick wobbled his way to the door and grabbed the handle.

It was locked! He jiggled it frantically, letting go of Mike to use both hands when the door remained firmly closed. He stared at the wooden roadblock, his mind a maelstrom threatening to pull him down.

"I thought you said Jo was waiting," Mike whispered.

"She is!" Nick snapped. "Or at least, she was. Just shut up and give me a minute." Anger surged through his veins, anger at Mike that quickly morphed into anger at himself for lashing out and for thinking he could trust someone. "Sorry," he mumbled, "I just need to think for a minute."

For lack of a better plan, Nick tugged again on the corroded brass handle. When nothing happened, he leaned his forehead against the heavy door before looking up at the small window. "Jo," he called softly. "Jo, are you out there?" *Please be out there*, he added silently.

He was turning to Mike in defeat when she finally answered, "Hang on. I'll unlock it."

Nick stepped back just as the door swung open on complaining hinges. "Let's get out of here," he said and once again grabbing Mike's hand, he stepped through the door and closed it behind them.

Her back to the dark hallway, Jo looked small but determined. "Hello, Dr. Sanchez," she said, aiming a pale grin at him like it was any ordinary day of the week in Colorado Springs. When Mike nodded a greeting, she aimed a worried look at Nick. "I heard noises, and I," she looked over her shoulder and took a deep breath, "I was afraid to leave the door open in case someone came, so I locked it and hung up the key. I'm sorry. I didn't know what else to do."

His pulse still pounding at the prospect of being locked in a prison, waiting on Shades, Nick muttered, "It's okay, no harm done. Let's just hang the—" He stopped abruptly, glancing at the door, the peg for the key, the hallway. He took the key from Jo. "Let's leave the door unlocked and take the key with us. We can throw it overboard when we go up on deck." He gave Mike a sideways glance. "It's not much, but maybe some of those guys will have a chance."

"Yeah, maybe," Mike responded with a voice that said he didn't believe it for a minute.

Jo moved closer to Mike and squinted up at him in the dark. "I'm so sorry about that other man, Dr. Sanchez. The one who was beaten," she said, and the sincerity in her voice made Nick's throat ache.

Mike blinked. "You saw?"

"Yes, sir. We both did." Wrapping a thin arm around Mike's waist, Jo snuggled up against him. Mike gave her shoulders an awkward squeeze as she looked over at Nick. "So, what now, Rockefeller?" The nickname was forced and out of place, but for some reason, it lifted Nick's spirits.

What *was* next? Finding Mike had been Nick's primary focus, but now, that goal had been met. He'd thought, he'd just assumed, that Mike would know what to do. His dad knew everything about everything. But, his dad simply looked stunned and speechless. That meant it was up to Nick. He felt the mantle of leadership land squarely on his shoulders with all the subtlety and finesse of an anvil.

Suddenly, he saw Miriam's face, heard her voice. She had told him he would have to learn on his own. That it would be hard. But she hadn't said it would be impossible, and despite all his bravado in front of Angus Dent, as far as Nick could tell, this was an impossible situation. And that wasn't his only problem. How was he supposed to learn to be a leader on his own when he wasn't 'on his own'? He had Jo and Mike to think about. If he failed, if he made a wrong decision, they would all pay the price.

Nick bit his lip, stalling, hoping Mike would take charge or that Jo would suddenly lead the way like she had up on deck earlier. But the two of them simply stood there waiting, their eyes on him. 'Hard things,' Miriam had said. 'It's up to you. You hold the key.' He stared down at the rusty key. He held a key all right, but not….

Nick grinned and took a deep breath. Letting it out slowly, he looked at his companions.

"What?" Jo said.

"You're not gonna like this, but…the Bosun." When she frowned, he added, "Mr. Amherst. We have to find him. He's got the coin and we have to get it back." As quickly as it had appeared, his elation left him.

What was he saying? They would have to face the Bosun, a beast of a man who would probably rather run them through with his bloodied knife or let Whistler have its way with them than have to deal with them. Not only that, there was the storm, and the Captain, and maybe even some

Shades along the way. 'Hard things.' What could be harder than facing down a Shade? His tired brain started to conjure up an evil Keeper — whatever that meant — who took pleasure from chopping off hands. And what about the Scribe who, according to Angus, was behind the Keeper's actions? What would he look like? A monster? Satan? Complete with horns and a pitchfork?

Nick shook his head to rid himself of the images before he lost his courage. Squaring his shoulders, he looked Jo then Mike in the eyes. "We have to," he ordered, even though neither Jo nor Mike had offered any objection.

With each step up the darkened stairway leading to the main deck, Nick's worries about the storm became more and more a reality. Lightning streaked across the narrow opening at the top of the stairs and thunder growled out a deep-throated warning that, each time, came moments too late. The ship thrashed like a mechanical bull, bucking forward then back, listing wildly to the left then the right. Sea and rain water tangled in harsh rivulets that poured down the stairs, making every footstep treacherous.

Keeping a tight grip on Mike's arm, Nick glanced at his dad. The muted light funneling down the stairway showed bruises on his dad's face. It worried him that despite with both his and Jo's help, Mike was struggling to climb the stairs. He knew his dad was doing his best and Mike had yet to voice any complaint after his earlier comments about being a bit stiff and having a headache. Still, a single ugly thought replayed itself again and again in Nick's mind: They were in trouble if Mike couldn't even climb a simple flight of stairs.

When they finally reached the last step, Nick glanced outside before tugging Mike towards the old hiding place under the tarp-covered barrels. Exhausted, the three of them awkwardly tucked themselves between the barrels and the ship's rail.

Nick took a second to catch his breath and brush water and wet hair out of his eyes. A glance at Jo said she was doing the same. Mike simply sat hunched and gasping.

Raising his voice to be heard above the wind, the waves, and the rain, Nick said, "Stay here. Rest." Jo, her face pale, looked up at him. "I'm just going to scout around. I'll be back in a few minutes," he yelled, adding a few gestures that he hoped would help Jo figure out what he was saying.

She nodded and mouthed, "Be careful," as she scooted closer to Mike.

Turning to leave, Nick heard his name. He looked back to see Jo and Mike huddled together with their arms wrapped around each other for protection against the storm. Mike seemed oblivious to Nick's leaving, but Jo gave him a wan smile. "Stay away from the railings, Fred Astaire," she murmured through the sheets of rain. Then added, "And watch yourself."

Raising his hand in acknowledgement, Nick slipped out from under the canvas and staggered into the full intensity of the storm. Grabbing handholds wherever he could find them, he used his free arm to shield his face from the stinging onslaught. Waves slammed into the side of the ship, breaking over the railing and splitting into twin rivers that disappeared around opposite corners of the large cabin that sat in the center of the deck.

Once past the protective walls of the lower cabin, Nick felt exposed, and not just to the elements. As he made his way forward, he looked around often and cautiously, but spied no one through the darkness of the storm. No wonder. 'Even the Shades have enough brains not to be out in this,' he thought and lightning marked his epiphany.

Time lost meaning as he slowly fought his way towards the front of the ship. He kept his eyes on a small enclosure built onto the forward deck. Too small to be much more than a storage closet, it still promised safety compared to being out on the open deck. He inched towards it.

Had he been gone ten minutes? Two? An hour? He had no idea. He wiped burning saltwater from his eyes. He was cold and more tired than he could remember ever being. Worse, the water seeped through his skin, leeching into his soul and weighing him down.

It was with a grateful sob that he finally fell against the side of the small structure. He pressed himself into the sodden boards, clenching his fists and resting his head against the rough surface. It took a Herculean effort to quell the trembling that wracked his entire body, and another not to wrap himself in a fetal ball of futility.

He wasn't sure what he expected to accomplish by making his way to the front of the ship. To be honest, other than knowing that he had to find the Bosun, he had no plan. Still, Nick was unprepared for what greeted him as he stepped out onto the deck of the Shade Runner's triangular bow and looked back towards the cabin and deck sitting halfway between the ship's large masts, towards where Jo and Mike waited.

He gasped as, through blurry sheets of rain, he spotted the lone figure at the ship's wheel on the upper deck.

Illuminated by the ghostly backlight of a sputtering, swinging lantern was the Bosun. Amherst was bound by a thick rope to the ship's wheel, preventing him from being swept away as he wrestled the storm-tossed sea. There was no sign of anyone else — no Shades, no crew, not even Captain Samael.

Realizing that the Bosun hadn't seen him, Nick's bravado returned. "Safe and warm in your cabin, hey, Captain?" Nick snorted with contempt. "Leave the crew to do your job. Some leader," he added just at the Shade Runner tilted at a crazy angle.

The ship groaned as she dropped into a cavernous valley between two monstrous waves. Nick had no time to brace himself. He heard a roar to his left and looked over just in time to spy a colossal wave, the Mother of All Monstrous Waves, rise up like a whale over the rail and bear down on him. Nick desperately fumbled for a handhold, but his fingertips slid across the soggy boards of the storage bin. His feet slipped out from under him just as the wave reached him.

He was swept away. His only thought was that, this time, he'd really bought it. No more sneaking out to movies when he should be studying. No more wondering what it'd be like to kiss Jo on the mouth. No more wishing that his family wasn't fractured beyond repair. No more wanting to track down Miriam to make her tell him everything she knew. 'No more anything,' was on his mind as he saw his legs clear the ship's railing.

Then he was screaming and...and not falling. Not drowning. It took a conscious effort to stop yelling. He looked up to find that he'd somehow snagged a section of the rail in a death grip. When the ship tipped again, the other way, he thought he might make it after all. But before he could pull his body over the rail and onto the deck, the Shade Runner rolled again and his body was lifted until he hung perpendicular over the ocean.

"Mike!" His fingers slipped a little, enough to terrify him. "Somebody help me!" He grimaced from the effort of hanging on. "Dad," he shouted, but even as he called out, he knew there was no way they could hear him.

The Shade Runner plowed the waves, continuing to lean at an impossible angle. His arms were being pulled from their sockets. Nick tightened his grip, fighting to hold on with the same inner strength that he'd kept carefully hidden beneath years of attitude, a leather jacket, and a fake lip ring.

"Let go." The voice was so close and so calm that Nick nearly lost his desperate hold.

Grunting, he tried to turn his head to look for the speaker, but the effort was too much.

"If you are the one," the smooth voice said, "let go."

Nick twisted wildly, trying to glimpse his rescuer. "Help me, whoever you are! I can't hold on much longer." To his right on the upper deck was the dark figure of Mr. Amherst, who fought to right the ship. To his left...

"Captain Samael," he whispered.

Standing less than five feet away, the Captain stared down at him.

CHAPTER 11

SPINNING DEALS

Captain Samael looked slightly amused. A ghost of a smile played on his face. His manner was casual, arms relaxed at his sides, and Nick couldn't help but notice that he rode the bucking ship with the grace of some super hero out of a movie.

Nick took another quick look around. Samael must have been standing at the very front of the ship the whole time, but even drenched from the rain and waves, he looked completely comfortable and in control. Other than the Captain and the Bosun two stories up, there was no else in sight. No Shades, no crew.

It took all Nick's strength to swing back around so he could look the Captain in the eyes. "Help me." His words were tossed aside by the wind and Samael's indifference. "Please," he begged.

"I can." Samael made a move as if he were going to step closer then he stopped. "But, perhaps, you should…." The smile faded and his brow wrinkled in concern.

Rain dripped off the deep brim of the Captain's hat. Nick blinked rain out of his own eyes waiting for the man to complete his sentence. When Samael didn't speak, Nick's patience slipped along with his grip. "What?" he screamed. "Perhaps, I should do what?"

"Let go."

"Let go?" Nick felt insane laughter building, but he refused to give in to it. "You can't…," he grunted with the effort of tightening his grip on the rail. "You can't be serious."

"Oh, but I am." The Captain looked past Nick, calmly surveying the skies as if he had all the time in the world. As if he were not standing idly by while a teenage boy clung to life, dangling bare inches over death's maw. When Samael glanced back down, a smile colder than the depths of the sea was back in its former place. "Surely, Eli will protect you. And He can certainly pluck you from a watery grave much quicker than I. See if I am not right. Put Him to the test," the Captain urged. "Let go."

Nick felt dazed, hypnotized by the smooth, sure voice. "Eli?" He turned his head, rubbing his face against his wet sleeves in an attempt to clear his muddied thoughts. When he looked back up, the Captain had cocked his head and wore a puzzled expression.

"Eli and Reuben," he spat. When Nick did not respond, he stated, "You do not belong here."

Nick could almost hear Jo reply, 'No kidding, Sherlock. What clued you in?' He, on the other hand, wasn't sure what to say. So, he said nothing.

Captain Samael chuckled. "All right." He straightened and lifted a hand towards the black storm clouds. "Then, whatever name you may give Him, test The Maker. He will save you, will He not?"

"I don't—I don't know." Nick blinked back tears of exhaustion and looked up at the raging storm. In the face of it, he was insignificant. Whether he lived or died, it didn't matter. The storm would continue to play itself out. Ships would keep sailing and the practice of gathering Shades would go on.

His life amounted to nothing. He was going to die a lost soul in a world where he didn't belong. His mother, his Grandma Carlota, his old friends, teachers, and classmates, no one would know what had happened to him. Some of them wouldn't even care. Some might even be a little happy about it. And, even the ones who would care would get over him eventually. Even his mom. A few months down the road, a day would pass when she wouldn't even think about him. Before the semester was over, someone would take his seat in geometry class. His clothes would be farmed out to a local thrift shop, dissipating amongst a city of strangers.

Grandma Carlota would probably remember him the longest. She'd try to tell his story, but no one would believe her weird tales about the grandson who'd inherited his grandfather's gift of traveling. The boy who was doomed to follow in Grandpa Fidel's shoes — a Traveler who simply disappeared, leaving no footprints as proof he'd ever existed or to point the way to where he'd gone.

"Let go, Young One," the Captain said, his voice taking on the tone of a command.

Nick squeezed his eyes closed, tears mingling with the biting rain. "Help me," he whispered. "Please." He heard cruel laughter, but ignored it. He wasn't pleading with the Captain anyway; the Captain scared him. The thought of accepting help from Samael sent a wave of revulsion and fear through him. A fear he didn't understand, that seemed stupid in light of his current predicament.

He waited, clutching the rail with fingers that had gone numb, and hoping for some kind of miracle. But nothing happened. He didn't feel any different. He wasn't snatched to safety. When he opened his eyes, he was still suspended above absolute death and a few feet to his right a Shade leered at him.

A Shade! Nick gasped.

The ghastly, deformed creature stepped up to the rail and leaned down, reaching out with its only hand. Panting from the exertion of hanging on, Nick's eyes slid to the thing's other arm, to the stump, and his mouth went dry. He licked his lips, but his voice failed him. Weak sparks of adrenaline warned him to let go, to escape, but he was too scared. Like a trapped animal surrounded by predators, he awaited the first fatal move.

If he'd thought to wonder if Shades breathed, he had his answer in the form of a puff of air that burrowed its way to him through the wind and stank like something buried then unearthed days later. One of the Shade's eyes — his right one — looked damaged, shriveled, and grey. Nick looked away, meeting the 'good' eye, but even it was cloudy and strangely warped. He shuddered when a bone-white, emaciated hand brushed across the skin of his arm.

"Who will you choose?" The Captain's voice startled Nick. The presence of the Shade had overshadowed Samael, and in the interim, the Captain had drawn nearer. His voice had taken on a fatherly tone.

The Captain now leaned against the rail, so close that Nick could see the intricate pattern of leaves that decorated the buttons on his jacket and smell a faint residue of tobacco. He found himself fascinated by a hangnail on the Captain's left index finger, the only sign of imperfection. But, his study was cut short when the Captain's jacket snagged on the rail, revealing a scabbard hanging from a black leather belt.

"You can join me," the Captain offered and Nick forced himself to meet Samael's gaze. The officer nodded at the Shade. "Or him."

Nick glanced at the Shade, at the Captain. Then back again. The Captain was a handsome picture of calm assuredness with a smooth voice, while the Shade was a cadaverous creature. Its limbs, its eyes, even its clothes, were mangled beyond repair. The two were polar opposites, both revolting in their own way.

The Shade growled something unintelligible through a throat full of gravel, dirt, and horrors untold. Words dribbled out on foul breath, splattering over Nick like lukewarm sewage. Words that sounded like, 'Poor sigh me own.'

Nick's cramped hands were slipping; his nails could find no purchase on the damp wood. If he didn't choose soon, there would be no choosing. It would be over. He closed his eyes, saying a silent good-bye to his mom, Mike, Jo....

"The Shade," Captain Samael whispered, "or me." When Nick looked up, the man was holding out a strong, clean hand.

"Poor sigh me own," the Shade garbled, trying to grab onto Nick's arm.

"Come, boy. Choose."

"Poor sigh—"

"You!" Nick snapped and grabbed onto the Captain's wrist with his left hand.

Samael's lips curled into a leer of victory, and immediately, Nick questioned his decision. Then, as if Nick weighed nothing, the Captain grabbed Nick's right hand and pulled him over the rail, dropping him in a heap onto the deck of the heaving ship.

The Shade's bony shoulders drooped even more as it turned its cloudy eyes upon Samael.

"He has chosen," the Captain said. Holding onto Nick, he waved his free hand at the Shade like he was chasing away a hungry seagull. "Go on. Be gone."

The Shade flinched and a hiss escaped it as it slowly backed away. The shriveled gaze fell upon Nick, and for a brief unbelievable second, Nick could have sworn he saw pity in the damaged eyes. Pity? For himself?

"I...I want...." The Shade might have frowned. "For you...." It huffed as if frustrated at its inability to communicate clearly.

Frustration. Pity. Nick's stomach churned at the thought that these creatures were capable of emotion. Prisoners of their own sorry, rotting flesh.

"Be...be coz sigh me own," the creature managed and raised its butchered arm as if lifting a severed hand in a good-bye wave. Striking its own emaciated chest with a wet thud, the Shade let the limb drop to its side in frustration and defeat. "Sigh me own," it repeated once again before shuffling towards the rear of the ship.

Through a curtain of rain, vividly aware of the cold fingers still clasping his right hand, Nick watched the Shade go. It was almost out of sight when its words finally sank in. "Simon," he muttered. He looked up at the Captain. "It was saying Simon, wasn't it? For Simon."

Samael gave a snort of amused indifference. "Was it? The creatures speak all manner of things. At least for a time. Their minds, if they have them, are not right. It's of no consequence."

"No, I think it—I mean he—I think he meant Simon. The kid that helped us."

"Us?" The Captain cocked his head again then squatted down next to Nick. His eyes narrowed, and he said, "So, it's as I thought. You are not alone."

Nick's heart sank. "Uh." His mind raced as he tugged weakly, and to no avail, against the Captain's hold on him. He realized he was trembling violently. He clenched his free hand into a fist in a failed attempt to quell the tremors. "No, I'm just...it's just me. I'm by myself."

Samael stared at their clenched hands before slowly releasing his grip. "You are with the one in the hold. The one dressed like yourself."

All Nick could manage was a single shake of his head.

"Which one of you is the Traveler?"

He gulped. "Neither."

Immediately, Nick felt like crying. Or screaming or barfing. Or, maybe, all three. He'd screwed up. With one simple word, he'd basically admitted that he knew what a Traveler was and that he and Mike were together. He moaned.

With deliberate movements, Samael stood and tugged on the collar of his dark jacket with its fancy buttons. He straightened his hat then looked out over the heaving ocean. The sounds of the storm had abated as if held at bay by the cloud of silence surrounding them.

Finally, meeting Nick's gaze, the Captain said, "I will tell you what I believe. I believe that you stole aboard to rescue the one below — a foolish, futile plan, by the way. I believe that your companion is a Traveler who will soon find himself face to face with the Keeper." Samael smiled. "I can hardly wait to see his covetous face when he realizes he has finally stumbled on the object of his obsession. Although," he let out a mock sigh, "I do hate to see the end of the Gathering." He shrugged. "Oh, well, as they say, all good things...."

Samael dipped his head slightly, allowing rainwater to drizzle from the brim of his hat before he continued. "I also believe that this Simon you speak of sold your soul, my young friend. I do hope he received ample reward." He smiled at Nick, a smile that was as sincere as Principal Demmick's when she'd welcomed Nick to Colorado Springs and said she looked forward to getting to know him. "And, finally," the

Captain said, "I believe that you are in my debt. Bound to me. Now and always."

"In...in your debt?" Nick managed in a bare whisper. "Bound?" Without thinking, he scrubbed the palm of his right hand against his jeans in an attempt to clean it of the Captain's touch. It didn't work. He could still feel Samael's grip.

The Captain stared down at Nick with eyes that burned with a sudden intensity. "Now and always," he repeated then walked with unnatural grace towards the rear of the ship as if Nick had served his purpose and was already forgotten.

Still sprawled on the deck, Nick looked up at the sky. He stared past the gulls huddled on the ropes and gazed into the stormy face of infinity, recalling Miriam's warning: 'There are pathways not even the falcon's eye has seen or the storm taken.' Her words still didn't make sense, but he felt as if the meaning was within his grasp. If only he weren't so exhausted. So hungry. So tired. He could lay here forever, despite the cold rain, lulled to sleep by the rocking of the ship.

He rolled his head to the side, looking out beyond the rail. What he saw caused his stomach to sink and his weariness to vanish. He sat up, rubbing rain and seawater from his face, hoping his eyes were deceiving him.

Cleared vision brought with it fear and dread, which settled over his shoulders like a rubber raincoat, numbing him to the incessant beat of the rain and the spray of the ocean. With a groan, he rolled to his hands and knees then clambered to his feet. He had to pull it together. Jo and Mike needed him, and their time was running out.

When Nick slipped into the hiding place, Mike looked more rested, and much to Nick's relief, he pulled himself slowly upright. A half-eaten apple and an empty plastic bottle testified that, once again, Jo's seemingly bottomless backpack had provided sustenance.

"Where have you been?" Jo demanded. Before Nick could snap that he and a few of the better looking Shades had been cruising for girls, Mike cleared his throat.

"So, what do you think, Nicco? What's our next move?"

Although it was strange having his father defer to him, something deep inside stirred, acknowledging his birthright as the one who should lead. Nick straightened his shoulders, trying to ignore the strange tingling in the palm of his right hand, and the guilt and shame that accompanied it. "The Bosun is at the ship's wheel up on top of the cabin."

"The helm at mid-ship," Mike supplied. When Nick cocked an eyebrow, he added, "It's called the ship's helm."

He stopped and a long, tired sigh escaped. "Sorry," he muttered. "Guess that doesn't matter."

"That's okay," Nick said, wondering how his dad seemed to know everything about everything. Was it because he was so educated or because he was so old?

"Then I guess we should go confront him," Jo said, her eyes big and scared. She hesitated before slipping the strap of her bag over one shoulder.

Nick reached over to stop her. His hand hovered momentarily over her shoulder before he grabbed the strap, pulling it from her arm. With a muffled thud, the bag hit the wet deck. Jo's fist clenched. "Why'd you do that?" she scowled at him.

They swapped squint-eyed glares before Nick blinked and looked away. "Will you just shut up a minute? There are a couple of things you guys should know." When they both looked at him, his fear and guilt hardened into something else. Maybe it was resolve, or maybe it was just hunger or the beginning of some alien intestinal flu. Whatever it was, he hoped the pain of it written on his face had translated into strength and self-assurance. "I think we've been found out."

He quickly told them about meeting the Captain, about Samael saying Mike was a Traveler. He left out the parts where he almost died and how it was because of him that the Captain reached his conclusion in the first place. And he especially omitted the part where he'd apparently struck some kind of deal with Samael.

"What was...how did...," Jo fumbled then frowned. "Why would he just let you go?"

Mike laid a hand on Jo's shoulders, silencing her. "Why not? Where could Nicco possibly go?"

Jo nodded. "I guess you have a point."

Mike was staring at Nick. "There's something else, isn't there?"

Nick hesitated, wondering if maybe he should just keep the news to himself, but an inner voice told him they deserved to know. "I saw land."

Could time stop? He supposed it could. After all, if a funny looking coin could transport them here, if one-armed zombies could sail ships, and if a horse-faced woman could change his life, he supposed anything was possible. He just wondered, because time seemed to stop for a minute after his revelation. Thunder ceased mid-rumble, no lightning flared, no gulls spied on them, the ship halted its rocking, and Jo and Mike stared at him without blinking.

Then Mike's Adam's apple bobbed up and down as if he were swallowing the news like a lump of unchewed meat.

The Shade Runner rolled and a jagged shard of lightning sliced open the clouds.

When his dad simply said, "Then we'd better hurry," Nick couldn't help but wonder which hand Mike would lose.

"Yeah," he mumbled.

"I wonder what made the Captain think there was a Traveler onboard," Jo said.

He glared at her. "Why are you asking me? How am I supposed to know?"

Jo frowned. "You don't have to be such a jerk." Her eyes raked over him as if scratching his surface to reveal any buried clues. "I was just wondering."

"Maybe he has the coin," Mike said.

Nick shifted his gaze to his dad, glad to escape Jo's scrutiny. He was happy to let them think that might be the reason for Samael's conclusion; besides, he hadn't thought about the Captain having the coin. "You think the Bosun gave it to him?"

"Or the Captain took it."

"Yeah, he seems like the type who would spy on people," Jo agreed. "He probably saw the Bosun with it and took it. Then again, the Bosun could be a brown-noser, so maybe he gave it to him hoping for lighter duty or a promotion. Who knows why he did it, but I'm bettin' he did."

Nick nodded, refusing to meet Jo's gaze. "You're probably right. Captain Samael probably has it."

"Then we should start with his cabin," Mike said.

Nick swallowed. "Yeah, I suppose so." Dread settled like a rock in his gut. He'd rather gnaw off his own toenails than have to chance another meeting with Samael, but he didn't want to say so. "Yeah, I guess we should search his room, but we need a diversion to make sure he's not in there when we do it."

"Good thinking, Einstein," Jo said, "but what if the coin's not in there, either? What if the Captain has it with him?"

Nick might have thought Jo was simply trying to deflate his plan, poke holes in it before it was even airborne, but one glance told him otherwise. Her query was a simple question, nothing more. A question for which he had no answer. "Then we'll move on to the next plan." He paused, raising his eyebrows. "What number are we on again?"

She grinned. "Dos? Tres? Does it really matter?"

"Not unless it's the last one."

"What happens then?" Jo looked like she was shrinking before his eyes.

Nick shrugged. "Then we all go home."

Mike broke the moment. "A diversion, huh? Preferably something that won't sink the ship."

"That'd be good." Frustrated and tired, Nick peeked out at the mast that had been his and Jo's shelter through the long night. "Any ideas?"

"I reckon I might be some help to ye."

Nick couldn't explain the relief he felt at the sight of Angus Dent's wiry figure squeezing under the tarp and into their cramped hiding place. It was like waking up in a panic because you hadn't studied for your second hour geometry test then realizing it was Saturday. It felt great.

Angus nodded at Mike and tossed a wink at Jo before smiling at Nick. "Sleight of hand be me trade, lad. Diversions be me very nature."

"You came back," Jo said.

"I couldn't abandon ye, now could I?" He tapped his skinny chest. "Me ole' heart wouldn't let me rest if some-thin' happened to ye while I be hiding away."

Nick wondered if that was the real reason Angus was here. Or was it because he was scared to be alone? Either way, they could sure use his help. "We need the Captain out of his room," he said.

"That be no problem, boy. Ye leave it to ol' Angus. I be fixing a right fine surprise for the Captain of this devil ship." He scooted back. "Ye will be knowing when the time be right," he whispered then slipped out as quickly as he'd slipped in.

Nick's thoughts were as cramped as his leg muscles. It was foolish to trust the old con man, yet he had no other ideas. No other options. So, the three of them huddled in their tight quarters, saturated to the point of being as withered as Grandma Carlota's roommate, waiting for an unknown signal from an ex-crimp. Was there such a thing as an ex-crimp? Not according to the ex-crimp himself.

Nick tried not to doze off, which wasn't easy despite the threat of discovery, his aching body, and the assault on his nose. What was that smell anyway? It was like a dead fish washed up on the shore and baking under a Chicago mid-summer sun, combined with the sour smell of a damp towel buried in a gym locker. He tilted his head in Mike's direction and sniffed. It wasn't coming from his dad. Maybe it was Shade BO. Or maybe it was—

"All hands!" Nick flinched at the loud cry. "All hands on deck!" It came from the back end of the ship and sounded suspiciously like a certain ex-crimp. "The Gathering be loose! Skins on the aft deck!"

A shiver ran up Nick's spine. Peeking through a slit in the canvas, he held his breath as the cabin door just a few feet away was slung open and the Bosun's dark bulk filled the frame.

Trying to free himself from the rope that had secured him to the ship's wheel, Amherst looked back over his shoulder, up the stairs. "Captain, a piece of the Gathering be on deck!"

"Stand aside, oaf."

Tangled in the rope, the Bosun stumbled from the door and fell to his knees, the habitual sneer knocked from his hairy face. Cowering in the shadow of Captain Samael, Amherst certainly didn't look capable of cold-blooded murder.

"If any of them make it to the railing, Mr. Amherst," the Captain said, "you'll be first in line to greet the Keeper when we dock."

"Please. Please, Captain," the Bosun mumbled when Samael rested a hand on the hilt of the sword tucked in the scabbard at his side.

"Get up, you useless waste, and gather the crew. I'll have both hands of whoever left the cell unlocked." He turned, his black eyes combing the area. Cold fear pricked Nick's spine as the familiar gaze rested on their hiding place. Then, almost casually, Captain Samael stepped over the Bosun and strode away. "Blow the horn, Mr. Amherst," he ordered as he headed toward the rear of the ship, "and call the Shades to cull."

"Aye, sir." Getting to his feet, the Bosun hurried to do his Captain's bidding. "Aye."

Nick and Jo exchanged a cautious glance as the sound of the storm gave way to three shrill notes and the tramping of numerous feet on the wooden stairs. Shouted orders and flying threats filled the deck. It took more courage than Nick thought he possessed to wait until the tramping ceased then toss aside their covering, dart across the narrow exposed area, and move up the stairs towards what he hoped was the Captain's quarters. He didn't dare look behind him, but he heard what he hoped was Jo and Mike on his heels.

A dozen steep steps led to a small landing. More steps led up to what Nick assumed would be the deck where the Bosun had steered the ship. To his right on the landing was a closed door. Letting his gut lead him, he opened the door and stepped inside. Jo and Mike followed him then he closed the door.

After his tour of the jumbled bowels of the Shade Runner, Nick was surprised by the tidiness of the little room. Running along the wall opposite the door was a narrow bed with a bookcase headboard that reached to the ceiling. Squeezed beneath a small round window that looked out over one side of the ship were a desk and wooden chair. Nick took it all in quickly and decided that the very orderliness of the room identified it as belonging to the ship's pristine Captain.

He looked at Mike, who was pale and bruised but uncomplaining. "Maybe you'd better sit down while we search the cabin."

"Search?" Jo looked around the tiny quarters. "That's not gonna take long."

Mike slumped down in the desk chair. "I'll look here," he said, already fumbling with the desk drawers.

Spying a trunk pushed into the corner, Jo knelt and began rummaging carefully through it.

"Don't worry about being neat," Nick advised. Climbing on the bed, he swept the books from the shelves in one violent motion. Leather bound volumes tumbled across the bed and hit the floor. "We've got to hurry. I don't how long Angus can stall them. Besides, they already know we're onboard. We've just got to find the coin."

"Yeah, I guess," Jo agreed and began tossing the trunk's contents over her shoulder.

Nick's back was to the door when it was flung open. He knew without looking and raised his arms in surrender. Their luck had run out.

He turned. Sure enough, Captain Samael filled the doorway, looking down at Jo then over at Mike. The man stepped into the cabin, giving a cursory glance at the wreckage as he nudged a book out of his way with a polished boot. "Mr. Amherst, join us." The burly Bosun stepped into the room.

Leaning down to retrieve a white shirt that Jo had thrown to the floor, Samael made a show of brushing it clean before tossing it onto the bed and gracing them with a tight smile. "It appears my young friend has brought his companions to meet us, Mr. Amherst." Despite his apparent calmness, seething anger leeched from the Captain, filling the corners of the room. Cold eyes settled on each of them in turn, Nick last of all. "Have you found what you seek?"

Jo still knelt before the trunk, Mike sat hunched in the chair, and Nick was standing on the bed. He lowered his hands, but otherwise they didn't move. None of them spoke, but the Captain didn't seem to care.

"If so, I hope it is worth the cost." His eyes never leaving Nick's face, he ordered, "Close the door, Mr. Amherst. We don't want these thieves to escape, now, do we?"

Still mute, Nick watched the door swing shut. The only other way out was the window. It was so small that Jo was the only one who might be able to squeeze through it.

As if thinking the same thing, the Bosun reached down, grabbed Jo by her braid, and pulled her to her feet. Nick tensed and Mike stood up.

"Let go of me, you stupid Neanderthal!" Jo punctuated her order with a bloody scratch that ran down the Bosun's hairy cheek like an exclamation point.

Amherst howled and cupped his injured face with his free hand. Samael looked amused as the Bosun pulled back his hand, preparing to strike. "I'll be teaching you some manners, wench."

Nick launched himself in Jo's direction just as the cabin door burst open, hitting Amherst in the back and causing him to stumble forward against the Captain. As Nick landed on his feet next to Jo, a bony figure stepped through the open doorway, a figure that caused hope to soar.

Caught momentarily off guard, the Bosun lowered his hands, his injury apparently forgotten, and turned on the newcomer. "And who, by the Scribe, be you?" Amherst spat.

The old man raised himself to his full height and smirked at the Bosun. "Be ye forgetting me so soon then?"

"Don't pretend you don't recognize the notorious crimp of Berken Bay, Mr. Amherst," the Captain said. Nick's new-found hope vanished when Samael smiled. "What kept you, Mr. Dent?"

CHAPTER 12

PUTTING A CRIMP IN IT

"Mr. Dent?" Jo's voice quivered and her disheveled braid, which had finally succumbed under the Bosun's rough hands, only added to her puzzled appearance.

Nick knew exactly how she felt, but when he spoke, it was anger that rattled his voice, not confusion. "You lied to us!"

"Aye, that be true. I suppose I did." If not for his persistent smirk, Angus Dent might have looked as contrite as he sounded. "But, I also be truthful, be I not? After all, who be telling ye that a crimp be a scoundrel that cannot be trusted? And who be warning ye not to believe anything a crimp be saying?"

"You, but—"

"And who be confessing to be a crimp?"

"Well, you did," Nick conceded.

"And yet, ye did not heed my warnings."

Nick and Jo shared a glance. It was true. In his own strange way, Angus Dent had given them ample warning.

"So," Angus said with smile, "it appears that ye be at fault yer own selves."

"But, if it weren't for you, we wouldn't even be here," Jo said. "You arranged a distraction so we could get in this room."

"You even helped us get in the room where they were holding the prisoners, so we could free my dad," Nick added.

"Nicco," Mike murmured, "you called me..."

He shot a quick glance at a frowning Mike. "What?"

There was a slight hesitation before Mike shook his head and said, "Nothing," in his 'we'll talk about it later' voice.

Angus Dent cleared his throat, and Nick's attention was pulled once again to the crimp, who paled under a glare from Captain Samael. Dent gulped then shrugged his bony shoulders. "I confess that I be having a wee bit of fun with 'em, sir."

"And with me, as well, it would seem."

"Oh no, Captain, sir. That not be it at all. It just be that...uh... well, you see...." It was obvious from the darting of his eyes that Dent's criminal mind was hopping from horse to horse in the middle of a rushing river. It was also obvious when his gaze and smile settled on Samael that he had decided upon the steed that he thought would take him safely to the far shore. "You see, my dear Captain, I be leading them straight to you, sir. Yes, that be what I did. I knew ye be wanting to talk to these little schemers. They be different. That you be—"

"Enough," the Captain ordered and in one swift move, he crossed the small room and grabbed a fistful of Angus's scant hair in a strange imitation of the Amherst/Jo scene of a few minutes earlier. Despite the fact that Mr. Dent had lied to them, had set them up, Nick couldn't help but feel a wave of sympathy when the Captain pulled Angus's head back at an impossible angle, forcing the old man to his knees.

A smile softened Samael's face, but Nick knew it was not a smile to be trusted. He knew that the Captain was armed with a sword that had lopped off who knew how many hands. As if reading Nick's mind, Samael flipped his jacket behind his scabbard and pulled the weapon free.

The sword sliced through the air like a living being, sucking the oxygen from the room and seizing every fragment of light in the small space, before coming to rest over the head of the crimp. All eyes were glued to the deadly instrument. Its elaborately engraved handle curled familiarly around the Captain's hand as if it, not the man, was the one in charge. Its honed edges glistened as if still damp from the blood of a half-dead Shade or salivating in anticipation of slicing through Angus Dent's exposed throat.

"Wait," Mike mumbled. Then he said it again, more firmly. When Nick forced his eyes from the scene playing out by the door, he saw that Mike was now standing between Jo and the Bosun and was staring at Samael. "Don't do this."

The Bosun's filthy hand dropped to the hilt of the knife at his waist and his gaze shifted back and forth between Mike and his commanding officer, waiting for the order to kill.

"Aye, Captain," Angus pleaded in a strained voice. "Listen to the man. He–"

"Be quiet," Mike snapped as if speaking to a disruptive student. Then, offering a tight smile and holding up a hand, he softened his voice as if reasoning with a schoolyard bully and not a full grown man armed with a sword. "Not in front of the children, please."

Clearly puzzled by the request, Samael said, "You do not want the children to see me kill this man."

Mike nodded. "That's right. If you must kill him then do it. But, let them go first. I'll stay."

"Hey!" Angus protested. "Do not be so eager to hand me over to the roaming lion."

"Shut up," Samael said with a tug on Dent's hair, and Nick wondered if the crimp was tired of being interrupted. "Tell me, Traveler, from which realm do you come?"

Mike frowned and threw a quick glance at Nick. "I don't know what you mean."

"Of course, you do," the Captain said and lowered the blade of the sword closer to Angus's neck. "Mr. Amherst, why don't you give our guests a peek at what they're searching for."

"Huh?" The Bosun gave them a blank stare.

Samael sighed. "I tire of these games, people. The cube, Mr. Amherst. The cube."

"The cube, sir?"

The Captain rolled his eyes then, for the first time since their meeting at the railing, he looked deep into Nick's eyes. "My young friend," he said with narrowed lids, "you have not forgotten our arrangement, I hope."

Nick blushed. Out of the corner of his eye, he saw Jo staring at him. He refused to look back. Instead, he studied his hands until the Captain ordered, "Come, Amherst. We haven't much time. The storm abates, and we'll soon lay anchor."

"But, sir, I do not know what ye want."

"The coin, man!"

Amherst stiffened and his grungy face went white as a Shade. "The...the coin?"

Samael snorted back laughter. "Who do you think you are dealing with? I saw you with it earlier," he said in a voice laced with warning.

Just when Nick was about to tell the Captain that he was wasting his time, that the Bosun was obviously as dumb as a box of rocks, something flashed across Amherst's ugly face.

"Oh, aye. The coin, you say?" the Bosun smiled. "Why, I be giving the coin to Mr. Dent."

"Dent?" Samael echoed in disbelief then stared down at the crimp. Angus still knelt with his head forced back. The sword brushed against the old man's Adam's apple. "I should have known. Ever a crimp, hey?"

Angus tried to shake his head, but the Captain's grip on his hair was too tight. "No, sir. He be lying."

"Where is it?"

"He be lying," Dent said. "I swear it!"

Nick gasped and heard Jo do the same when Samael pulled so hard on Angus's hair that the crimp's knees came up off the ground. The sword's edge pressed into the wrinkled neck spawning a thin stream of blood that disappeared inside the collar of Angus's filthy shirt. When Mike took a step toward the Captain, Amherst drew his knife and blocked Mike's path.

"Where?" Samael demanded, shaking Dent's thin frame. Angus wrapped his hands around the arm which held him.

"I do not be having it." He struggled to breathe, to speak. "He lies, I tell ye." With a final, violent shake, Samael tossed Angus away from him. Dent hit the wall hard then slid to the floor in a boneless heap.

"Stop it!" Jo screamed.

The Captain stepped up beside the pitiful crimp and pressed the tip of his sword against the scrawny, heaving chest. "I be giving it to you, Captain," Angus managed. "If'n I had it. I swear by the Scribe."

The tip of the sword sank half an inch into Angus's chest. While the old man screamed in pain, Samael turned his head and glared at Amherst. The Bosun was eyeing Mike, so it took a moment before he realized he had his commanding officer's full attention.

"You will all be meeting the Scribe if it is not handed over to me," the Captain announced to the room at large. "Immediately."

"I swear it," Angus gasped, "on me own dear wife's grave."

Nick remembered the discussion of the house in the valley by Berken Bay and Angus's loving wife and family. Was Angus's wife waiting? Was she dead? Was he ever even married? Which story was true? He didn't know what to believe.

"I be swearing it, too." The Bosun's voice trembled. "I be giving it to the old man right after we be raising the sails. He told me he be coming as yer agent." The hand holding the knife shook and Amherst's bloodshot eyes silently pleaded with his superior officer. "Captain, why would I be lying to ye?"

Samael met the gaze. His manner was emotionless as he steadily rocked with the sway of the ship while one hand pressed firmly on the handle of the sword piercing Dent's chest. "Why indeed," he finally stated with a voice that Nick knew could just as easily order the death of each and every one of them.

"You," the Captain suddenly snapped. Nick flinched as if struck, but Samael was looking at Jo, not him. "Search the old man."

"Me?" Jo said.

Samael inclined his head, once again a Southern gentleman.

Jo inched forward. She made her way past Amherst, scowling and reaching up a hand to pinch her nostrils closed.

Nick felt an ill-timed, out-of-place chuckle building in his throat, but it never saw the light of day. Instead, it dropped to the pit of his stomach when the Captain grabbed Jo's shoulder with a strong hand.

"Search him well, daughter, or I will carry you to the feet of the Scribe myself. Perhaps the hand of a girl will appease the old lecher."

Nick heard Jo gulp. When she nodded, Samael released her and she dropped to Angus's side.

"Mr. Dent," she murmured, "are you okay?"

The sword sank further, accompanied by a worrisome popping sound. Angus gasped and tried, unsuccessfully, to get up. Jo looked up at the Captain, tears running down her cheeks.

"No talking," he ordered. When she made no move, Samael patted her on the head with his free hand then gave her a firm shove. "Search."

Nick was entranced by Jo's crying. It was absolutely silent, evidenced only by the hitching of her shoulders and the tears that splattered onto Angus Dent's prone form. Gentle fingers explored the pockets and corners of the crimp's clothes. She even leaned close and ran her hands along the collar of his shirt and through his matted hair. Her quiet, "It'll be okay,

Mr. Dent," muttered to an old man who was now bleeding from the mouth appeared to go unheard by the murderer who watched them both.

Resting a small hand on Angus's shoulder, Jo glared up at Samael through a film of tears. "He doesn't have it. He doesn't have anything," she said. "Are you happy?"

Samael smiled down at her. "Sublimely," he replied casually then leaned his full weight onto the sword.

Jo and Dent both screamed. Nick ran over to join them. Samael pulled his weapon free and kicked Nick as he went by, otherwise he ignored them. Barely aware of Mike yelling at Samael, Nick landed roughly on Jo's backpack which still rested on the floor near the door. Crawling to Angus's side, sitting across from Jo, Nick felt tears of his own building as he stared down into the man's pale face. Glazed eyes settled on Nick and bloodied lips moved.

"What?" Nick leaned close, pressing his ear to the man's mouth. "What is it, Mr. Dent?"

The only thing he heard was a soft 'baa' sound.

Nick touched the crimp's wrinkled face and nodded. "I remember, sir. Berken Bay." Nick sniffed back snot and tears. "Don't worry, I'll find them. I'll find your family."

Angus shook his head, a move so slight it might have gone unnoticed if Nick's hand hadn't been resting on the forehead. Dying eyes blazed out an unspoken plea, and Nick pressed his ear close again.

"Baa." A puff of warm air followed the sound then, almost imperceptibly, the old man uttered his final words. They were simple. Two words. Two syllables.

Puzzled, Nick sat up. He glanced around. Jo sat across from him, grasping Angus Dent's dirty right hand and silently crying. Samael stood in front of the Bosun and Mike stood nearby. Nick saw anger hardening his dad's jaw as Mike eyed the two men.

By the time Nick looked back down, Angus Dent was dead. The sword must have cleaved the old crimp's heart completely in two. For all of her tears, it might have done the same to Jo. His eyes on the Captain, Nick reached out and blindly fumbled with the snap on a pocket. Fingers sought and searched. Just as he began to lose hope, he found what he was looking for. He must have gasped when his fingers closed around the prize because Jo looked over at him. Her eyes were swollen and her nose was red.

"What are you doing?" she whispered.

With a subtle move, Nick revealed to her what was clasped in his hand. Jo gave a grim nod and smiled through her tears.

"The bag," Nick whispered back. "That's what he said. He knew where it was all along."

Jo looked at Angus's still face. "Then he must have put it there. But when?"

Nick shrugged and glanced over at the men. "Who knows. But, you know what that means?"

He watched as the Captain pressed the tip of his sword against the Bosun's broad chest. Amherst stared down at the weapon that still dripped with Angus's blood. He seemed to have forgotten that he held his knife because his arms dropped limply at his sides and his face went pale.

"Stop," Mike ordered in a voice that lacked its usual authority. "You can't do this." But Nick had a feeling his dad was wrong. He had a feeling that Samael could pretty much do whatever he wanted.

As if to prove Nick's theory true, the Captain ignored Mike. "Where is it?" he asked his underling.

Amherst shook his head. "I be giving it to him. I tell ye, I be giving it to him for ye."

His eyes blurry with unshed tears, Nick felt an evil grin take possession of his face. "It means the Bosun isn't lying," he whispered to Jo and a thrill went through him to think that the man who'd committed cold-blooded murder himself just a short time ago was facing his own death. And Amherst didn't even deserve it, not for this anyway. Just like Angus Dent hadn't deserved it.

"Be searching me," the Bosun pleaded. He began to pat himself as if to prove that he wasn't hiding anything. "Let me be sh—"

"I'll do it," Mike said. "I'll search him." And he stepped closer to the men.

A strong hand snapped out and grabbed Mike by the collar. "Nice try, Traveler," Samael growled.

"What?" Twisting against the grip on his shirt, Mike frowned at his captor then at Nick, who rose to his feet.

Still holding Amherst at bay with the sword, the Captain pulled a struggling Mike closer until their noses nearly touched. "Who do you think you're dealing with? You would like nothing better than to get your hands on the cube, but you will not. Not while I'm in command."

"I—I don't know what you mean," Mike mumbled, flicking a glance at Nick and Jo.

"You're going nowhere. Except with me. As soon as I deal with Mr. Amherst," Samael grinned and nodded his head in Jo and Nick's direction, "and the children, of course. Then you and I are headed to the Keeper's." He chuckled. "I can hardly wait to see the Scribe's wily old face when I toss you at the feet of the Keeper. It will be..." Samael chuckled again as if he couldn't contain his joy. "It will be, quite literally, his undoing."

"Hey, Cap."

His dark eyes still dancing with mirth, the Captain looked over at the speaker.

"Is this what you're looking for?" Nick held up the coin.

Samael frowned. "Where did you get that?"

"I be telling you," Amherst gasped.

Nick felt a strange power run through him. "This is what you want, right?" he taunted.

"Nick, don't," Jo whispered.

"Hand it over," the Captain ordered.

"I be telling you!" The Bosun glowed with righteous indignation. "I be—"

Whatever he was going to say was silenced by the Captain's yell to "Shut up!" and the simultaneous jab of the sword that pierced the filthy shirt and sank into Amherst's fat belly. The Bosun screamed in pain and dropped to his knees, but Samael didn't even glance his way. Still holding Mike with one hand, the Captain kept his eyes on Nick.

"Hand it over! It can do you no good." To underline the order, the sword hand raised.

When the blade pressed into the flesh of Mike's throat, everyone in the room froze, even dying Amherst, who gasped out his last rancid breath.

A loud clap of thunder, the loudest yet, rolled across the surface of the sea and pounded its way into the ship. It shook the timbers, rattling the vessel and causing even the sure-footed Captain to struggle for balance. Nick watched in stunned fascination as the deadly blade nicked Mike's neck. The sight of his father's blood spurred Nick into action

"Let's just see what good it can do for me," he said and squeezed the coin in his palm, desperately wishing himself home. All he could do was hope and pray that Mike and Jo would be sucked back to Colorado Springs with him. He didn't know how the cube worked. If he had to be within a certain distance from them. If everyone around him would be swept up with them. He hoped not. He certainly didn't want Samael standing in the middle of their living room wielding a bloody sword.

It took a moment to realize that nothing was happening. Nick opened his hand and stared down at his palm, wondering if he had the right coin.

The Captain laughed, and Nick felt the blood rush to his cheeks.

"What?" Jo said, wiping the last of her tears and snot from her face.

"I don't know. Miriam didn't exactly explain how—"

Samael's laughter immediately stopped. "Miriam?" When Nick gave him a puzzled look, the Captain released his hold on Mike to hold up a hand. "About so high. Crazy red hair. Kind of, well, horse-faced."

Nick nodded, stunned. "How do you know her?"

"No," the Captain murmured, looking between Nick and Mike, "the question is, how do *you* know her?"

Out of the corner of his eye, Nick saw movement. Before he could turn his head to look, the door flew back on its hinges and he heard the screech of an entire crew of shattered voices, the strangled cries of the half-dead crying out for vengeance. For justice.

The Shade who'd tried to rescue him at the rail, Simon's father Laban, crossed the threshold first. He lurched towards the Captain, followed by a stream of one-armed monsters who all stumbled in the Captain's direction chanting, "Skin, Skin," over and over like a baleful prayer. Nick saw blood and gore smeared on the faces of a few of the Shades, and he wondered briefly if he was seeing the remains of the prisoners or of the Captain's human crew, or both.

Samael stepped backwards across the room, stumbling over the prone form of the Bosun. Mike moved out of the way of the Shades, hurrying towards Nick and Jo. Nick's eyes were glued on the Captain, so he saw clearly the sliver of doubt that appeared like a fault line along the officer's chiseled jaw.

As Laban reached the Captain, he glanced back at Nick. The Shade's mouth opened as if he wanted to speak, but then he turned away and lunged at Samael.

Vaguely, Nick heard Jo gasp and felt Mike's arms stretch around him, but his attention was drawn to the warmth of his palm and the red pulsing of the cube. Sucked into the protective void of the bubble, he raised his eyes and met those of Samael. The Captain's glare was pure evil combined with something else.

Triumph?

Then there was nothing.

They found themselves not in Mike's comfortable family room, but in Grandma Carlota's bathroom. They were huddled together a few feet away from the haggish old roommate who sat on the toilet amidst a rank stench. The old woman stared at each of them in turn before reaching for the roll of toilet paper.

"Uh–" Nick struggled to escape, fearing what was about to happen almost as much as he had feared the Captain of the Shade Runner.

Mike frowned, straightened his disheveled shirt, and nodded politely. "Excuse us, ma'am."

Jo burst into tears. Nick could relate. In fact, as the woman reached for the hem of her gown, he thought that if they didn't get out of the cramped room immediately, he might sob a little himself.

"Jo," Mike said softly, "it'll be okay. We're safe now."

But Jo shook her head and pressed her face into her hands. "No, it won't, Dr. Sanchez," she sobbed through tears and grimy fingers. "That was my favorite backpack."

Epilogue:
An End And A
Beginning

Nick's fingers kneaded the bedspread into uneven lumps as he sat on his bed staring at the faded picture in the cheap frame on his desk. He studied the washed out image of his grandfather. "Grandpa," he said softly, testing the word. Displeasure wrinkled his forehead and pulled down the corners of his mouth. The word tasted sour on his tongue.

"Fidel." Nick nodded. That was better. It was easier to call his ancestor by name. It made his connection to his grandfather feel distant, slightly unreal, just like the image of the serious looking man in the photo.

"Where are you?" he asked the stranger gazing steadily back at him with dark eyes. Nick was surprised by the tears which suddenly stung his eyes. He wiped them away in one harsh swipe.

They'd been back for over a week now and he was still having trouble controlling his emotions. At least Grandma Carlota wasn't alone now in believing that Fidel was alive, that he was out there somewhere. Even Mike admitted that his father might be trapped on the other side, perhaps trying to get home. That he hadn't abandoned them, not intentionally anyway.

Nick tensed at the thought of Mike. The hug his dad had given him after their escape had caught them both off guard. It had been awkward yet natural. They'd stepped out of that smelly bathroom and their shoulders had brushed together. Mike had startled Nick by hesitantly throwing his arm over his son's shoulders and squeezing him roughly. "It's true, Nicco," he'd whispered. "He's waiting for us to find him."

Grandma Carlota had cried, at first from the shock of three people stumbling out of her bathroom. Then she'd shed real tears when Mike announced that he believed her about Fidel. She'd thrown her arms around Mike and sobbed into his shirt collar. Unconsciously, Nick touched his own collar and discovered not tears of joy, but a piece of limp broccoli. He smiled as he looked at the latest missile from today's visit. If Grandma's roommate ate as much broccoli as she threw, it would explain the smell in the bathroom.

Nick grunted softly, astonished that not only did he find the broccoli funny, he wanted to share the revelation with Jo. He was pretty sure she'd see the humor in it. He was also fairly certain that something had changed — was changing — between him and Jo. It had only been a week since their return, but he didn't really hate Jo any more, maybe just disliked her a little.

Digging in his pocket for his new phone, Nick's fingers snagged the chain instead. Pulling it out, his smile died. He stared at the metal disc attached to the serpentine chain, studied the praying hands on one side of the medallion. Turning it over, he read the tiny etched letters: 'God grant me the serenity to accept the things I cannot change; courage to change the things I can; and wisdom to know the difference.'

It seemed stupid now — taking his dad's necklace. He no longer cared about causing trouble between Mike and Grandma Carlota, and he knew he needed to return the jewelry. But, that nagging voice in his head had been planting the same seeds of doubt for the last week: His dad was just starting to accept him, maybe Mike even liked having him

around a little, and if he found out Nick had stolen his necklace, he'd never trust him again.

"It's not worth the risk," he decided once again. It would
be safer to pretend he'd found the necklace somewhere, or
simply sneak it back into Mike's room for his dad to find. That
way, the necklace was returned and he didn't get blamed.
No harm, no foul.

Problem solved, Nick pulled out his phone, but the urge
to call Jo wavered as he punched in the number. His finger
hovered over the last digit. His mouth tasted like a sand dune
in the Sahara. If he called her, he might look desperate and
she might not even find the broccoli story funny. He should
wait. Nick shoved the phone back in his pocket and walked
into the bathroom to get some water.

"Nick," Mike yelled from the kitchen, "supper's ready."

Ignoring his dad, Nick stared at himself in the mirror.
Dark eyes peered through the thick, black hair masking half
his face. Grandma was right. He did have Fidel's eyes — the
eyes of a Traveler. A proud smile tugged at the corners of
his mouth.

He was a Traveler, and he had a sneaking suspicion that
there'd be other journeys.

Hadn't Miriam said as much when she'd met him in the hallway after his return? "The path of the cube is one of faith, Nicholas, and if you are faithful to follow it, there is no blame. The passage price has been paid by Eli's son. By Reuben," she'd said, touching her hand to her chest, over her heart.

"Eli. Reuben." Nick mouthed the old-fashioned names and a strange shiver raced up his spine. Although his darting eyes assured him he was alone, he couldn't shake the feeling that he was being watched. It was the same feeling that had haunted him all week, even when he was at school.

Then, as he stared into the mirror, the feeling was replaced with an unexpected anger. It was all riddles, especially Miriam's talk about following a path of faith and not having blame. Why would she say that? If she could read his mind — if she knew he blamed himself for everything that had happened — then she ought to know that Nick wasn't good at trust or faith. After all, what reason did he have to trust anyone or have faith in anything? As far as he was concerned, getting blasted into another world was easy compared to the whole trust thing. And, who or what was he supposed to trust anyway? Miriam? Mike? Himself? The coin? Someone named Eli that he'd never even met?

It was a lot to think about, and he wasn't sure he wanted to. After all, he'd trusted Simon, which had been a mistake. He had a sinking feeling that he'd screwed up again when he hadn't trusted Laban, but had trusted Samael instead — at least when his life had depended on it. He could still see the triumphant sneer on Samael's face as he'd grasped Nick's hand at the rail. "You are in my debt. You are bound to me. Now and always." Nick shuddered and rubbed his palm.

He kept waking up each night with dread pressing down on him and overcome by the feeling that someone or something was watching him in the dark. The first time it had happened, he'd thrown aside the covers — and his tough guy image — and had raced down the hall to Mike's room. But, as he'd put his hand on the doorknob, his father's soft snores had stopped him. Obviously, Mike's sleep wasn't being disturbed.

Coming to a decision, Nick had sighed deeply. He'd straightened his shoulders, marched back to his bedroom, and had started leaving on the bathroom light — even though he wouldn't admit it. It wasn't the first time he'd faked courage, but behind the false bravado, the unease lingered. It was a sickening feeling that something was lurking, hiding around the corner, slinking into shadows, and waiting for the perfect moment to pounce and tear him apart.

Nick swallowed a hard lump of fear. Over the last week, he'd come to believe that you didn't have to see something to know it was there. Like the necklace, which he'd tried to hide and forget about, but couldn't. Like Samael's taunt about being always in his debt, which was another thing he'd been shoving in his pocket to deal with later. But, there was something else even more insistent than the stolen necklace or the Captain's gibes — it was a wrinkled face that invaded his thoughts, a raspy voice that demanded an accounting, and tormented gasps that wouldn't be silenced even by death. It was Angus Dent of Berken Bay.

Nick stared at his hands, but he saw blood pooling on a cabin floor. Should he have trusted Angus? Had Angus betrayed them or saved them? Would things have ended differently if Nick had chosen Laban? He didn't know. He only knew that he felt he had cost the old man his life, and he was pretty sure Mike and Jo blamed him, too. Worse, Angus had known it during the last terrifying moments of his life.

Miriam was crazy to talk about having no blame.

Spying his new lip ring on the counter, Nick picked it up. He rubbed the cool metal between his fingers then hesitantly laid it back down.

Mike's impatient call interrupted his internal debate. "Nicco, now!"

Nick slipped the fake piercing onto his lip, twisted it to just the right angle, and smirked at his image in the mirror. "Okay, okay. I'm coming!"

ABOUT THE AUTHORS

Judith K. Gallagher — As a mother of five and a veteran teacher, Judith Gallagher has an extensive background working with children and teens. Her passion is sharing her love of writing as she unlocks the author in every child. She has written numerous educational articles, short stories and poetry, and has spoken professionally at the county and state levels. She and her husband, Jim, are enthusiastic travelers. Tempest is her first novel.

V.C. Warren — Vicki Warren was born and raised in Missouri, and has worked as a paralegal and a hearing officer. After living in Colorado for many years, she now lives in Central Missouri with her husband, Jake. An avid reader, she has been writing short storises and poetry since the age of 9. Tempest is her first novel.

Author Contact: Judith.Vicki.books@gmail.com

CPSIA information can be obtained at www.ICGtesting.com
Printed in the USA
LVOW01s0420060815

449075LV00015B/136/P